SADDLER'S WELLS

SADDLER'S WELLS

RUSS THOMPSON

A Black Horse Western

ROBERT HALE · LONDON

ISBN 0 7090 6001 7

Robert Hale Limited
Clerkenwell House
Clerkenwell Green
London EC1R 0HT

Photoset in North Wales by
Derek Doyle & Associates, Mold, Clwyd.
Printed and bound in Great Britain by
WBC Book Manufacturers Limited,
Bridgend, Mid-Glamorgan.

1

Saddler's Wells

The Indians had several names for Saddler's Wells, an ancient spring with shards, bones and burned rocks whose origin had been lost centuries earlier.

The spring filled a decent-sized pond and there was evidence of prehistoric people, called *Anasazi* which simply meant 'the old ones' had scratched crooked little ditches probably with stone tools or fire-hardened sticks to bleed water to patches of mottled corn, squash and other edibles. But although those artefacts turned up regularly, Saddler's Wells had within recent memory been a place where freighters camped, where buffalo hunters cured hides until eventually the only business establishment, a harness works founded and operated by an old man named Samuel Saddler, gave the settlement its present name.

Sam Saddler had been dead many years before his hamlet became a town, complete with an emporium, a gun works, a saloon, old Samuel's leather shop, even a physician's office upstairs over the fire hall.

The last Saddler, to folks knowledge anyway, was old Samuel's grandson, Ambrose, killed during a drunken brawl near the south end of town where a man named Rowe had just established a livery, trading and freighting barn.

There were conflicting stories about that fight. The shockleheaded liveryman-trader *et al*, said he knew nothing until gunfire awakened him, and by the time he got out back old Samuel's grandson was face-down-dead and the smell of whiskey was strong enough to make a brass monkey weep at a hundred feet.

They buried Ambrose, beside old Samuel, and life resumed its customary tenor, except that now there was no leather man at the Wells. Ambrose had been the last; inheritor of old Samuel's trade.

Liverymen and freighters required a saddle and harness works, mostly because they took no care of leather and, while it was tough, it did not stand being flung in the dirt by tired men forever. Mostly the townsfolk of Saddler's Wells shrugged about that loss, they were traders, storekeepers and the like who only indirectly relied upon freighters – harness men.

Outlying stockmen, though, along with freighters, came in time to wish another leather man would arrive and, when none did, after a couple of years, someone, no one was certain who, ran an advertisement in two newspapers for a leather man, one was in Albuquerque, the other in Denver.

The burly Greek who ran the saloon, Saddler's

Wells Drover's Rest, Christopholous Spartas – known simply as Chris – was of the opinion that given the size of the town, it would be a long time before a replacement for Ambrose would be found; a good leather man would make five times as much money up in Denver or down in Albuquerque than he could possibly make at Saddler's Wells.

Folks listened to Chris Spartas, not because he was particularly sagacious but because he had a voice like a foghorn, gestured with both massive arms and, after a pronouncement, would lean on his bar, black eyes challenging anyone to argue. Men went to the Drover's Rest to relax, stay cool in a semi-desert country where summer lasted almost until Christmas, maybe to drink, play pedro or poker and gossip, not to argue. It was this attitude which made it possible for the burly Greek to win most arguments – before they started.

Actually, Spartas was liked; he had a heart as large as a boulder, had a rough sense of humour and was known to save dregs which he poured into bottles for the old gaffers in rags who could not afford the price of a drink.

He and the individual bringing on a livery-trade-freighting business at the southern end of town, were close friends. They did not agree on the mystery of Ambrose Saddler's killing but Rowe at least had been down there, the first to find the riddled body, and therefore he had an edge when he and Chris argued. The liveryman's ultimate rejoinder was always the same: 'You wasn't there, Chris, an' I was.'

Rowe, whose first name was Willie, had been in

the Saddler's Wells country since the days of hide hunters; he was tall with a mop of greyish-white hair. He had been known as 'Rattlesnake' for years. No one reacted so violently to the sight of a rattler. To local knowledge Rowe had never been bitten, but as Doctor Morton said, a man didn't have to be bitten to dread rattlesnakes. It was something inborn. For a fact Willie Rowe had a pathological fear of rattlesnakes. Why anyone with that problem settled in a place like Saddler's Wells, New Mexico Territory was anyone's guess. New Mexico, so the story went, was where God, when he finally released the Devil, made a requirement of that release that Señor Satan could never go beyond the territorial limits, and he probably hadn't, but he kept busy. He created scorpions, sidewinders and diamond-back rattlers, hairy tarantulas as large as a man's hand, plus an endless variety of creatures that bit, stung, sucked blood, caused rashes, and ants that lived in the ground, emerged when annoyed, and had a semi-poisonous bite.

These things probably would not have been considered insurmountable, but New Mexico Territory was mostly desert where rainfall rarely arrived, where graze withered almost before making seed heads, and where there was water was invariably not where, for the best interests of people, it should have been. Also, if a person wanted to know where not to drink he simply had to look at the dozens of bleached skeletons. Poison water-holes were not common but neither were they rare.

Cattlemen brought in drives for the two to three months of graze then returned north. A few cow outfits, mostly owned by people with Spanish names, had been in the Saddler's Wells country for generations. They had controlled the water for more than a century. They also ranged herds over the only decent grass country, mostly hundreds of miles north of the New Mexico–Old Mexico boundary. The closer one got to the border the poorer, meaner, and more hostile the Territory became.

A stage company which had never granted a franchise south of Raton, maintained two way-stations, one north of the Wells, one south, closer to the border. The southerly way-station had mud walls three feet thick and, during the raiding season, kept a gun-guard on the roof. Mex marauders came often and departed swiftly in clouds of dust and gunfire. Except that the stage company had government contracts to deliver supplies and mail south of Saddler's Wells, it would have abandoned the southerly way-station long ago.

It was this reluctance on the part of the stage company to expand its interests south of Saddler's Wells which had given Willie Rowe the idea of establishing a business that could serve the territory neither the stage company nor anyone else wanted to serve.

Rattlesnake had once driven coaches for the stage company. He was as good a reinsman as he was terrified of rattlesnakes, which meant he was a topnotch *reindadore*.

He rarely visited Chris's saloon; the energy required to establish his dray, livery and livestock trading business kept him as busy as a cat on a hot tin roof. But, because Saddler's Wells, like most towns, thrived on gossip, Rattlesnake heard it all, perhaps not as soon as others, but soon enough, and once he was able to be the origin of a kind of gossip that stirred local interest.

It happened one early morning, about sunrise, when he was atop his barn replacing roofing the wind had torn, and saw the solitary rider coming from the east. The idea of patching roofs early was simply because once the summer sun got high, a man had to wrap his knees with croaker sacks to avoid burns, and if he persisted up there he risked heatstroke, and Willie was not a man who welcomed risks. But this time, while it was still cool, he put aside his sack of nails, put the hammer down, lifted his hat to mop off sweat, and watched the distant horseman.

Solitary riders were not unusual. This one was; about a mile behind him, whether he knew it or not, there were five Mex *bandoleros* stalking him, using underbrush, rocks, even the occasional piñon tree, for cover.

Willie shook his head. Those marauders were getting too close to town. Often when they came wild-riding from down in Mexico they were drunk. These men did not act that way, they were more like Indians. They rode too slowly to raise dust, and were only visible between places of concealment.

Willie had an urge to stand up and wave his hat. The man being stalked was too distant to hear a shouted warning. But as those shadowy *bandoleros* got closer, probably because they knew the town was not far, Willie slithered down his ladder, ran into the harness room and emerged in the back alley with his Winchester; not a carbine, a long-barrelled rifle. It could empty a saddle at almost twice the distance a carbine could and accomplish the same thing.

He was sweating as he emerged from the alley behind his barn, hurried diagonally across the broad main thoroughfare, got among the shacks at the farthest end of town, ignored the startled looks as he hurried past, and when he was beyond the farthest shack he stepped into shade squinting for a sighting of the solitary rider being stalked.

What the stranger did made Willie's breath hang up for a moment. The man would normally be expected to lope the last mile or so but not only did he not pick up his gait, he paused near a blowsy old cottonwood tree, and rolled a smoke.

There was no sign of his stalkers; there wouldn't have been, their kind could out-stalk Apaches, who were the best stalking killers west of the Missouri River.

What happened next kept Rattlesnake frozen. The stranger finished his smoke, stamped on it and swung into the saddle. All this was normal, but he did not continue toward town, he booted his horse out in a belly-down run. The first shot was to his left, where a few yards farther along a *bandolero* stepped from behind a rock, carbine rising. The stranger fired once, the *bandolero*'s gun went off skyward as he fell. One *bandolero* slid down the side of a tree, his weight breaking off a branch as he fell. Another *bandolero* sprang astride his horse and cruelly spurred the animal into a dead run, its rider low over the horse's neck.

A heavy-set *bandolero* dropped to one knee to aim. The stranger's third shot struck him head-on. He went over backwards, fingers scrabbling in the dirt.

The fifth *bandolero* stood up, flung his Winchester away and raised both arms high. The stranger rode to within four or five yards before he fired.

Old men came tumbling from their shacks. They, like the liveryman, stood like statues. Farther out, the stranger shucked out casings and plugged in fresh loads. What fascinated Rattlesnake Rowe was that the stranger's horse did not panic when the man on his back fired his six-gun.

One of the ragged old scarecrows with faded, pale eyes spat aside and quietly said, 'I never seen the like.'

The old men lingered in shade to watch the stranger resume his ride toward town, but Rattlesnake did not linger. He returned to his barn, leaned the rifle aside and sat on a bench in the runway. When the stranger appeared somewhat later Rattlesnake returned the man's nod and went to take the reins. The stranger was not a large man, nor was he young, Rattlesnake guessed him to be in his forties.

People were ganging together on both sides of the road. Few, if any, had witnessed the gunfight, but everyone had heard the shooting.

The stranger watched Rattlesnake stall his animal and said, 'A bait of grain, if you have it.'

'Rolled barley?'

'Fine.' The stranger went up front and stood in the doorway. He said, 'Saddler's Wells?'

Rattlesnake, busy graining the horse, answered shortly, 'Yep.'

'You been here long?'

'A while. I worked stock until a few months ago, then set up this business. Do some liveryin', but mostly freightin' an' tradin'.'

The stranger returned to the shade of the runway, sat on the bench outside the harness room and watched Rattlesnake fork feed to his horse. 'It's changed,' he said quietly, and because Rattlesnake did not know how to reply, he said nothing.

'Friendly town, is it, Mister …?'

'Rowe. Willie Rowe. Folks call me Rattlesnake. It's a friendly place.' Rowe went to share the bench with the stranger. 'I was patchin' the roof, saw you comin' an' saw some Messicans stalkin' you.'

The stranger had deep-blue eyes, almost violet in colour. They went to Rattlesnake's face and remained there. 'They been trailin' me since early mornin'. I'm not sure why but I can guess.'

'I'm not sure I'd have waited as long as you did,' Rattlesnake told the stranger.

The other man leaned far back then snapped forward. 'Bad back,' he said by way of an explanation. 'It worried me for a spell; they had carbines so I kept a good distance between us. They had chances to make a run on me.' The stranger smiled a little. 'There isn't a horse in Messico that could keep up with my thoroughbred. They didn't do it right; they kept stalkin'. When I stopped to have a smoke I was facin' in their direction. That would have been the time to make a run on me. Five to one. They were likely good at burnin' towns, killin' women an' old folks.' The stranger shifted his gaze to the heat-shimmery roadway. 'Mister … what was your name?'

'Rowe. Willie Rowe. They call me Rattlesnake.'

'Mister Rowe, when you run at 'em, they don't shoot straight. Mostly they're damned poor shots. Worse when they're full of *pulque*.' The stranger stood up. 'Those sons of bitches get full of liquor an' ride like the wind, killin', plunderin', stealin', burnin', an' when the liquor wears off they do other things. There are some things in this life a man don't need, bitin' horses, kickin' mules, cranky women an' *bandoleros*.'

The stranger stood a moment, then shoved out his hand. 'Sam Saddler, Mister Rowe.'

Rattlesnake came up off the bench wide-eyed. As they shook hands Rattlesnake said, 'There used to be some folks hereabouts named Saddler. I always heard because they did saddle and harness work that's how the settlement got its name.'

Sam Saddler's quiet smile reappeared. 'It was their name, for a fact.'

'Ambrose Saddler …?'

'My pa. My ma took me with her when she left him because of his drinkin'. We went back to Texas to her folks.' The gentle smile lingered. 'I told myself that someday I'd come back to Saddler's Wells.'

Rattlesnake, recovering from his shock, dryly said, 'Well, Mister Saddler, I got to say, when you ride into a town you let folks know it.'

Saddler asked about a place to stay. Rattlesnake sent him to the home of a widow-woman named Harris who took in folks. And after the stranger departed Rattlesnake headed for the Drover's Rest.

Everyone in town knew there had been a shooting, but for the first time Rattlesnake had the full story, and it made a deep impression the way he told what had happened.

The Greek set up a drink for Rattlesnake, on the house. He downed it, nodded his appreciation and the part he had saved for the last, he now told a silent room full of men.

'His name's Sam Saddler. His grandpa was the old man who founded this town. I always figured the town got its name from what old Samuel did for a living ... it was his real name. Sam Saddler was his grandpa. Ambrose was his pa.'

A dark-eyed man in the rear of the room loudly groaned. 'He's come here over what happened to Ambrose?'

Rattlesnake did not reply. Such an idea had not occurred to him, but when he finally spoke he said, 'Gents, he killed four *bandoleros* an' I saw him do it.'

The dark-eyed man groaned again. But this time he simply left the saloon without speaking. But what he had done made an impression. Men lined up along the bar, mostly quiet, mostly solemn as owls.

One man turned to ask Rattlesnake a question. 'Why was they stalkin' him?'

Rattlesnake replied the only way he could. 'I don't know. All he said was that they'd been stalkin' him most of the day, and that he kept out of carbine range of 'em.'

Rattlesnake's revelations moved swiftly throughout town. A few stockmen who had been in the saloon carried the stories to outlying areas. Like all small communities Saddler's Wells thrived on gossip.

The day after the gunfight an old man rounded

up the *bandoleros'* horses and brought them to the livery barn to be kept until a feed bill made it legal for Rattlesnake to sell them at auction.

They also buried the dead *bandoleros*, not happily, not even with a blessing. What was looted from their pockets paid for the digging of the graves with a tad left over to stand a round at Chris's place for the diggers.

2

The Unexpected

Aside from the shootout there were a number of
things about old Samuel's grandson that interested
the locals. For one thing he was soft-spoken,
friendly and likeable, which, Doctor Morton
crankily observed, was probably the kind of man
John Wilkes Booth, the assassin of President
Lincoln, had been.

Saddler paid the rooming-house woman a
month in advance, and when that got around
people assumed, with reason, that Saddler
intended to stay, and that increased local interest.

What ultimately, along toward the second week,
increased local interest was when Sam Saddler paid
cash for the building which housed the local
apothecary, whose business had never been more
than marginally profitable. But that was not the
interesting part; that building was the original log
structure where old Sam Saddler had had his
leather works.

Rattlesnake Rowe, who contracted to care for the stage-company's business, plus his own involvement with saddlery and harness, was one of the first customers of the re-established Saddler's Leather Works.

Rattlesnake became more of a local source of interest through his association with the latest Saddler to settle in the community, and was often enticed to the Greek's saloon and questioned about that association.

For one thing. Chris Spartas's patrons wanted to know, was Sam Saddler a genuine leather man, to which Rattlesnake could attest affirmatively because he'd taken bridles, saddles and harness up there to be repaired.

By the third week of the second month with Saddler being more or less accepted as a member of the town which had derived its name from his namesake and long-dead grandfather, even the Chinee caféman, who was not fond of round-eyed people, spoke favourably of the harness maker.

It was inevitable that Saddler's quiet, calm and friendly personality ultimately assured his acceptance. Nor did it detract that he proved himself a thoroughly knowledgeable and competent leather man.

One thing, however, stuck in folk's craws: one man shooting it out with five renegades, killing four and surviving without a scratch.

Arthur Carlyle who owned the local emporium, a bird-like man with a minimal personality, heard all the talk and without taking anyone into his confidence, wrote letters to several states requesting information about a man calling himself

Samuel Saddler. Carlyle signed each letter as town marshal of Saddler's Wells, which could have proven awkward when replies came in, except for the fact that his general store was also a federally sanctioned post office. He could therefore sort mail before others saw it, but as time passed he received either no replies to his letters of enquiry, or got back answers stating that the name and description supplied in his letters did not fit those of wanted men or fugitives.

If Chris Spartas had known of this, he would have bellowed in outrage, nor would he have been the only one. It was the custom of small towns to eye strangers askance. Those who lingered became victims of gossip and some pretty wild imaginations. But after five or six months, provided they did not do anything that upset folks, they were gradually accepted as part of the community, and Sam Saddler minded his business, did good work, his charges were reasonable, and because of his easy, friendly manner he was adopted as part of the business and social community. Nor did it hurt that he was the grandson of the old Samuel Saddler from whom the town had derived its name. If it intrigued folks that a perfect stranger should come to Saddler's Wells – in a blaze of gunfire – and turn out to be the grandson of old Sam the leather man, well, life was full of surprises, and what in hell difference did it make anyway? None.

When the stockmen who drove herds south to graze off the quick spring feed were preparing by mid-summer to go back north where it rained and feed grew taller, several cowmen and their riders came to town for supplies and to pick up horse gear from Sam Saddler's shop.

One of these cowmen was a grizzled, leathery-hided man of indeterminate years by the name of Frank Watson. He had a bloodless slit of a mouth, close-spaced pale eyes and a slight stoop occasioned by a hard life and age. Watson was a testy, irritable individual who usually brought two or three of his riders to town with him, two on the wagon he hauled supplies in and one man, a slaty-eyed, expressionless, tall individual who could stand perfectly still in one place and exude menace. His name was Alton Fisher; he was old man Watson's rangeboss.

It was not only customary but also inevitable that driving cattle over considerable distances using a wagon for essentials, and spending several months working livestock, that horse equipment either wore out or required replacement parts, or, at the very least, a sound cleaning and oiling.

Frank Watson had left a badly abused set of double harness at Sam Saddler's place to be cleaned, oiled and patched well enough for the long haul back up north, and Sam had done exactly as Watson had requested.

Maybe, as folks said afterward, old man Watson had too much bile, something old men seemed to acquire, or maybe it was just his natural capacity for being disagreeable, but whatever occasioned it when Sam brought forth the reconditioned and repaired driving harness, Frank went over each tug by hand, examined the britching by holding it to the roadway light, even went so far as to test collar pads to be certain they fitted correctly.

Sam leaned on his counter watching. When old

Frank made a snide remark, Sam did not respond. He smiled.

Alton Fisher, standing by the iron stove did not take his eyes off Sam for a long time; he was clearly categorizing Saddler by his responses to old Frank's complaints.

When Watson was finished he leaned on the counter fixing Saddler with a gimlet stare as he said, 'How much do I owe you?'

Alton Fisher crossed to the counter to shoulder the harness. His back was to the roadway door when Sam answered quietly, 'Six dollars.'

Old Watson reacted as though there were fire ants inside his britches. 'Six – dollars?' He put a thin-skinned, scarred and bony hand atop the pile of harness. 'Fellers like you figure because you're the only leather man around.... Up in Durango the charge wouldn't be no more than two dollars.'

Alton Fisher straightened up a little, put his cold stare on Saddler and for a fact he was an intimidating individual. Nor did it lessen that impression that he wore his holstered Colt low and thonged to his leg.

Without haste Saddler straightened up off the counter. He glanced once at Alton Fisher, then put his full attention on the older man when he said, 'If you're hard up, Mister Watson, I'll take five dollars.'

Watson reddened. 'Hard up? I can buy an' sell you out of my watch pocket.'

'Six dollars, Mister Watson.'

The cowman turned his head slightly and Alton Fisher stepped clear of the counter. Again Sam briefly considered the tall, intimidating individual before he said, 'Six dollars....'

'Or what?' Watson exclaimed.

'I'll keep the harness to sell for what I got in it.'

Watson also stepped away from the counter. He was red to the hairline. He softly said, 'Al!'

Fisher slowly lowered his right hand until the fingers brushed his six-gun.

A harsh voice spoke from the doorway. 'Pay him what you owe him, Mister Watson, an' tell your friend there to take his hands away from the gun.'

Watson turned but Alton Fisher did not take his eyes off Sam Saddler. Watson addressed the man in the doorway with a short-barrelled shotgun in both hands. Watson sputtered. 'You damned idiot, this don't concern you. Point that scattergun away. *Do it!*'

Rattlesnake not only did not point the shotgun away, he deliberately hauled back one hammer. 'Put six dollars on the counter, Mister Watson.' Then, as though expecting some reaction on the part of the cold-eyed, tall man, the liveryman and horse trader, said, 'Take your hand away from that pistol.' Rattlesnake cocked the second barrel. Frank Watson seemed to be holding his breath; seconds passed. On the far side of the roadway people passed in both directions. If any looked in the direction of the leather shop Rattlesnake Rowe's broad back would have blocked their view.

Frank Watson returned to the counter, pulled forth a long leather purse, pushed up from the bottom, extracted a crumpled wad of greenbacks, counted out six dollars – twice – and put them atop the counter as he jerked his head for Alton Fisher to pick up the harness.

As they left the shop both Fisher and Frank

Watson put long, bleak stares upon the liveryman, passed out into hot sunlight and angled in the direction of the supply wagon being loaded over in front of Carlyle's general store.

Rattlesnake waited until Watson and his companion were at the wagon where two of Watson's riders were loading supplies, then faced around and found Sam Saddler smiling at him.

Rowe said, 'Everybody knows that stingy, cranky old bastard. I was comin' up to see if you could make a boot for this shotgun.'

Saddler continued to smile. 'Good thing you came,' he said.

Rattlesnake leaned aside the shotgun, went to the wood stove, filled a tin cup with coffee from the pot atop the burner, and Sam Saddler said, 'Your hand is shakin'.'

Rattlesnake tasted the coffee. It was strong enough to float horseshoes. 'That shotgun wasn't loaded,' he said, and put the cup aside.

Saddler's smile disappeared. With his head cocked slightly he said, 'Do you play poker? Because if you do, let me tell you, from experience, the best way I know of to get hurt is to run a bluff like you just did.'

Rattlesnake's reply was a trifle sharp. 'An' if I hadn't come along – what?'

'I'd have taken the five dollars. Here,' Saddler held out a bottle from the shelf below the counter. 'It'll steady your hands.... I'm obliged, Mister Rowe. I owe you one.'

Rattlesnake took the leather man's advice, tipped whiskey into the coffee which made it cool enough to drink, and half drained the cup before placing the scattergun on the counter as he said, 'A leather boot for the thing. I got a habit of carryin' it with me when I'm haulin' freight.'

Saddler eyed the gun, it was old, the stock was scarred and if there had ever been any bluing on the metal parts it had been worn away long ago.

Saddler said, 'You got to be real close if you use that thing.'

The leather man's calmness irritated him, so Rattlesnake's reply was tart. 'I want 'em closer'n a couple hundred yards like you did.'

Saddler's smile surfaced, he took the scattergun to his work table and left it there. As he was turning back he said, 'As a friend, Mister Rowe, don't ever run a bluff with an empty gun.'

Rattlesnake's annoyance went up a notch. 'I won't, Mister Saddler. Next time I'll go over to the store an' buy some slugs an' come back.'

Saddler laughed. 'My name is Sam. Yours is Rattlesnake. I'll have the shotgun boot for you in a couple of days … an' Rattlesnake, I never forget a favour – or a wrong.'

When Rattlesnake left the leather works he strode southward in the direction of his barn on the west side of the road. Opposite the general store four rangemen stood impassively watching him pass.

Rattlesnake might have told this tale at the saloon, certain it would earn him a free whiskey. The reason he never mentioned it was fundamental. When he would have finished the story there would have been a room full of expressionless faces staring at him. Only a complete idiot would brace old Frank Watson and his gunfighter with an empty gun.

Autumn was approaching by the time Sam

Saddler had widened his acquaintanceship to include folks in town plus quite a few stockmen. His business prospered. Old Doctor Morton, who had a spinster daughter, went out of his way to make sure his daughter, Marianne, and Sam Saddler met at church socials, Fourth of July picnics, and the infrequent dances held upstairs over the fire hall in the large community room adjacent to Doctor Morton's office.

Marianne was not entirely unattractive. Few females were who were in their prime twenties, and she was both nice and personable.

What Enos Morton was up to would not have long remained his secret even if he hadn't been so obvious, but Marianne was well liked, as was Sam Saddler.

Doctor Morton, who had kept arm's-distance from Sam Saddler primarily because he did not much cotton to strangers, but also because, as a former Confederate soldier with scars to validate his survival of four years of combat, he was uncomfortable with the way Saddler had arrived in town; with four dead renegades and one survivor fleeing for his life.

He once told nervous Art Carlyle only a seasoned gunman could have accomplished what Sam Saddler had done.

But the first time his daughter shyly asked about Saddler. Enos Morton had recognized the symptoms and because people with ulterior motives can always find excuses, Doctor Morton closed his mind to what Sam Saddler had done to those *bandoleros* and embarked upon his mission of finding Marianne a husband.

At the autumn church raising – it was inevitable that God in the form of Southern Baptists should ultimately arrive in Saddler's Wells – Rattlesnake, Chris Spartas, an Orthodox Greek whose religious views were cheerfully slatternly, stood beside the local blacksmith, his helper and several cowmen who happened to be in town on that particular day, to raise the first, second and third walls.

Church raising like barn raising was a community affair, usually followed by picnics, playing horseshoes, and not infrequently music.

Rattlesnake, whose eyesight at distances was exemplary, but who had terrible close-vision, missed a spike and struck his wrist.

Doctor Morton was taken from some congenial locals who had providentially smuggled hard liquor to the church raising to look at Willie Rowe's wrist.

During a cursory and exquisitely painful examination by Morton who was not noted for gentleness and which in this instance was made rougher than usual through the influence of John Barleycorn, the pronouncement was a possible broken bone or at the least muscle damage, a prognosis concurred in by the local blacksmith, a man whose self-proclaimed knowledge of all things including bowed tendons, ringbones and thrush in horses, by his own lights entitled him to qualify with a second opinion.

The doctor took Rattlesnake with him to his office above the fire hall, bitterly complaining every step of the way about the clumsiness of Rattlesnake which had compelled him to leave his friends among some trees where they escaped attention.

While he was re-examining the wrist and considering treatment the doctor made an idle remark about the physical strength of Sam Saddler, to which Rattlesnake said, 'He's a good man to have for a friend,' and the doctor turned with a roll of bandaging in his hand and regarded Rattlesnake steadily.

'You a friend of his?'

'Yes.'

'A close friend, Rattlesnake?'

'We been close friends since he rode into town months ago.'

The doctor straddled a stool to begin the bandaging. 'Seems like a feller his age'n all ought to be married. Is he?'

'Not that I know of. He never said an' I never asked.'

'But you could find out, eh?'

Rattlesnake fixed his gaze on the medical man. 'If you want me to ask pointblank, I can't do that.'

'No. Folks don't ask personal questions. But you could maybe bring it up sly like.'

'Does that gawddamn bandage have to be so tight?'

'Any looser'n you'd be able to bend the wrist. What I should do is make a plaster cast for it. Only I haven't had no plaster in years. Now then, stand up. Hurt does it?'

'Yes it hurts.'

'Don't use that hand for liftin'. Don't put any strain on it. It'll likely be a month or better healin'. Did you ever think about gettin' eye-glasses?'

'What for? I can see as good as you can.'

Doctor Morton stood holding what remained of the roll of bandaging. 'A damned groundhog can see as well as I can. You owe me two bits.'

Rattlesnake forked over the coin, returned to the roadway with the sun sinking, the skeletal church walls up, braced and spiked into place, and standing alone where dozens of people had been.

His arm hurt. Instead of visiting the saloon he started for the lower end of town where his barn, shed and corrals were located.

He had chores to do, the kind that required two hands. As he passed the leather works Sam Saddler came to the doorway. Rattlesnake explained about the bandaged wrist and Saddler said, 'I'll get my hat. It takes two hands to do chores.'

As Rattlesnake dawdled, shadows lengthened, buildings showed either no lights or lots of lights, and the roadway as well as the sidewalk duckboards were empty. It was suppertime.

Rattlesnake heard the harness maker close the door behind him and turned. The explosion was loud and followed by glass flying where the window behind Rattlesnake and slightly to his left had been.

Saddler said, 'Get down!'

Both men flattened waiting for the next shot, which did not come, but the first shot had made enough noise to arouse a number of people. Two more shots sounded but were fainter.

Across the road the big Greek was holding a shotgun as he bellowed from his saloon doorway, 'Run for it. I'll cover you.'

They ran, burst past the spindle doors and nearly bowled over an old man holding a big hawgleg pistol. The old man staggered to a chair and sat down. Rattlesnake, Sam Saddler and Chris Spartas ignored him as they exchanged questions and answers. Not until they were at the bar with Chris gazing past them did anyone heed the old man. Chris said, 'Leonard, what're you doin' with that pistol?'

The old man ran a sleeve beneath his nose before replying. 'I missed the son of a bitch.'

The men at the bar stared. The old man arose to approach the bar. He shoved the big old horse pistol down the front of his britches, leaned looking steadily at Chris, who groped for the bottle of dregs from beneath the bar, filled a jolt glass and shoved it forward. The old man called Leonard tipped his head, dropped the liquor straight down, grimaced and said, 'I went out back to pee. There was two of 'em. They was gettin' a-horseback. The big one seen me watchin' 'em an' fired at me as his partner jumped out his horse. He missed; his horse was faunchin' all over the alley. I hauled up an' shot back. Missed too, I guess because he sat forward, gigged his horse an' the last I seen of 'em they cut westerly out of the alley.'

Leonard pushed his little sticky glass forward. Chris refilled it as he said, 'The one that shot at you was facin' you – who was he?'

As before Leonard downed his jolt before speaking. 'I don't know his name but he's that tall, mean-lookin' son of a bitch that's always keepin' company with Mister Watson, that cowman who drives down every spring from up north.'

'Was Mister Watson the other one?' Rattlesnake asked and Leonard shrugged bony shoulders.

'That one never looked back. I didn't see his face, but I sure-Lord recognised the tall one.'

Chris refilled the jolt glass for the third time but Sam Saddler reached to push the glass away as he shook his head at the Greek. There was no need for an explanation, on the floor where old Leonard was standing a widening pool was spreading.

The big Greek was in favour of getting a-horseback and going out where the Watson cow camp was. Sam shook his head. 'They'll get back before we can get close, an' the old man'll have all his riders lined up like crows on a fence.'

Rattlesnake said nothing. The exertion, excitement plus dropping to the duckboards earlier, had his injured wrist throbbing. He favoured doing nothing until morning. The others agreed. Too much time had passed anyway.

3

Reconnoitring

Rattlesnake's entire arm was swollen by morning, and painful, so the Greek and Sam Saddler left town the following morning without him.

They were an unlikely pair. Chris Spartas was forceful, direct, loud and powerfully opinionated. Sam Saddler was quiet, thoughtful and unexcitable. As they rode, Sam smiled, even laughed a time or two, at the same time his narrowed eyes below a pulled-low hatbrim missed nothing, unsure whether Chris was sufficiently experienced to suspect, because old Leonard had recognized one of the would-be assassins, and Watson would be expecting retribution, that the pair of townsmen could very well be riding into an ambush.

It was a beautiful day with larks in the grass, a few puffy white clouds drifting in an immeasurable expanse of turquoise sky. Visibility was perfect and while the land they rode over was for the most part grazing country there were occasional bosques of trees and flourishing man-high thickets of underbrush.

Sam chose a course which avoided stands of trees and the thick growths of underbrush.

The Greek, a confirmed townsman, had lived in the Saddler's Wells country for many years, but knew little of the outlying countryside.

Sam did not know the territory. As it turned out he was not required to; they were six or seven miles from town when they began encountering drifts of cattle, all wearing the same brand, a large FW on the left ribs.

Where they paused at a creek to remove bridles, loosen cinches and tank up the horses the Greek abruptly said, 'Well, well,' and pointed.

There were four horsemen approaching the far side of the creek from the south-west. Sam and Chris snugged up cinches, bridled their animals, then stood watching. The four riders did not hasten their approach. When they were close enough Sam recognized Watson's rangeboss, Alton Fisher. Chris said nothing but in his opinion the oncoming riders were not only armed to the gills, but were clearly not friendly.

Where they drew rein, about a hundred feet from the men standing with their horses, Fisher said, 'You fellers want somethin'?'

Sam replied quietly, 'We were lookin' for Mister Watson's camp.'

'Why? You're trespassin' an' Mister Watson don't like trespassers.'

'It's open range, isn't it?' Sam replied, and the tall, menacing individual loosened in the saddle without taking his eyes off Saddler. 'Not where we

graze, it ain't. You gents get back on them horses
an' ride back the way you came.'

Neither the Greek nor the loose standing man
nearby made a move to get astride. 'We'd like a few
words with Mister Watson,' Sam said.

'Would you now, an' what about?'

Sam smiled. 'It'd make it easier if we only had to
say what we come to say, just once.'

The three weathered, unsmiling companions of
Alton Fisher were seasoned rangemen. They sat
with both hands atop their saddlehorns. Their kind
did not have to see trouble coming, they could
sense it and wisely did not move.

Fisher looped one rein and swung to the ground
with the other rein in his left hand. 'Mister
Watson's real busy. We're fixin' to make a gather
an' head north.'

Saddler hung fire briefly before speaking again.
'I guess the grass is gettin' short for a fact, but we'd
like to settle somethin' before he leaves.'

'Settle what?'

'I just told you I don't like havin' to repeat
myself. You gents want to ride to the camp with
us?'

A grizzled Watson rider leaned and hissed.
Fisher turned. The rangeman jerked his head. He
and Alton Fisher conversed briefly before the
rangeboss swung back facing Sam and Chris.

Fisher studied Sam Saddler over a period of
silence before jerking his head. 'We'll lead the way,'
he said, and swung into the saddle.

As Sam and the Greek were turning to mount,
Sam winked. Chris did not wink back. Something
had happened he did not understand, but as the

riders turned south-westerly Chris allowed no one
to ride behind him.

It wasn't much of a ride, maybe a mile or a tad
more, and before they saw the wagon, the rope
corral and the grimy tents, they smelled smoke
from a breakfast fire.

Cattle were in all directions. Evidently the gather
had begun several days earlier. There were two
men in sight near the lowered tailgate of the
wagon, whose ash bows showed like ribs beneath
the patched wagon canvas.

Sam was not interested in the man at the tailgate
with a full beard, he kept his gaze fixed on the
leaner, sinewy older man.

When the riders dismounted to tie up, one of the
hard-faced rangemen growled when Chris was
preparing to tie his animal. The man said, 'That's
my spot. Tie somewhere else.'

Chris looped his reins and faced around. The
rangeman stood with his horse, glaring and hostile.
Chris said, 'I never told you where to stand at my
bar.'

'This here is different.'

Chris straightened up. 'No different. You want
to tie up here, try it.'

Old man Watson spoke to his rider while
crossing from the wagon. 'Leave it be!'

The hostile rangeman led his horse away and
Mister Watson took a wide-legged stance facing
Sam and Chris. 'We're busy. Whatever you got to
say make it short.'

Sam obliged but first he said, 'Whichever one of
you sons of bitches tried to bushwhack the
liveryman last night is a lousy shot, an' there's the

matter of a busted window. It'll cost about five or six dollars to get another one.'

Aside from Watson and furry-face at the tailgate who was not wearing a sidearm, there were five armed and stone-faced rangemen standing like they'd taken root.

Frank Watson gave his head a curt, disbelieving shake. He looked steadily at Sam. 'You come all that way an' rode into my camp to say you expect me to pay for your damned window?'

Sam smiled. 'Somethin' like that, Mister Watson. Maybe Mister Fisher didn't tell you, but him and an old gaffer in town traded shots in the alley last night, and the old man recognized your rangeboss.'

That grizzled, leathery-hided rider who had spoken to Fisher back yonder walked up to Mister Watson, whispered, and returned to his place between the wagon and the hitch rack.

Watson looked at his rangeboss. Fisher barely inclined his head. Watson faced Sam again and said, 'We wasn't in town last night. These boys'll swear to it.' Watson groped deep in a trouser pocket, brought forth a crumple of greenbacks, peeled off six of them and held them out. 'For your winder, from the goodness of my heart, because neither me nor Alton was nowhere near town last night.'

Sam tucked the notes in a shirt pocket, turned his back on Watson to swing into the saddle, and again winked at the Greek. This time Chris winked back. But as they left the camp Chris had to fight hard to keep from twisting to look back. Graveyards were full of victims of back-shooters.

When the men from town were beyond sight old

man Watson, his rangeboss and the bearded rider
talked together for at least fifteen minutes before
the old man stamped away yelling for his riders to
get astride, they had a gather to complete.

Chris, normally a gregarious individual, put one
or two sidelong glances in Saddler's direction but
when he finally spoke they had rooftops in sight
and whatever the Greek's earlier thought, when he
could discern his locked-up saloon, he groaned.
Business was rarely good in the morning, but
shortly now customers would be drifting in. It was
along towards dusk when they reached town and
put up their animals.

Spartas made a beeline for his saloon and when
customers arrived he had a tale to tell that baffled
his customers; one smiling man backing down not
just old man Watson, but his riders and menacing
rangeboss as well.

The tale lost nothing with each retelling. Doctor
Morton heard several versions and sat in his office
almost a full hour. Marianne was the apple of his
eye and the leather man seemed to be an ideal
prospect for a husband, but there was some
nagging wariness that prevented Enos Morton
from resuming his earlier role of matchmaker.

What his daughter thought mattered, of course,
but her father began to wish old Sam's grandson
had never arrived in Saddler's Wells. Under the
circumstances a wish of that kind was a waste of
time.

When Sam went to the emporium to give Art
Carlyle the measurements of a new window he
wanted the storekeeper to order for him, Carlyle
accepted the measurements but did not commit

himself to placing the order until he had explained that glass windows were expensive, one that size would cost at least five or six dollars.

Sam fished forth the crumpled bills, spread them flat and smiled. Carlyle agreed to place the order but admonished Sam not to expect the window to arrive in Saddler's Wells for at least four or five weeks.

Sam returned to his shop, rigged a white sheet over the window hole and cleaned up the mess. The sheet allowed light to pass through but of course no one could see in nor out.

Rattlesnake appeared a few days later, most of the swelling gone from his wrist and all the pain, not to admire the window covering but because he had heard the story of Sam and the Greek's visit to old man Watson's cow camp. Rattlesnake said he regretted not going out there with Sam – which was a lie – and congratulated Sam on how well he had come off from that encounter.

As the season advanced although the days were longer they were also hotter. Doctor Morton sent Marianne on an extended visit with his sister in South Carolina and his sister's brood, who were more or less the same age as Marianne.

There was a murmur of regret about leaving but Doctor Morton assured Marianne she would enjoy the trip as well as her kinfolk, the only kinfolk Doc had.

He neglected to tell her that former Confederate states, under the merciless heel of Union officers who served as administrators, were no better a decade or so after the war than they had been during the final year of the war.

Doc's motive was simple. One warm summer evening he had overheard Marianne and two friends talking about, and giggling over, the man they considered the most handsome and the most eligible bachelor in the territory.

Doc, who was not a serious drinking man, found no pleasure in coming home to an unlighted, cold house and, being a sorry example of a cook, spent time between the saloon and the rooming-house where the widow Eunice Harris, also lonely, and an excellent cook, fed Doctor Morton for slightly more than the Chinee caféman charged but there was no comparison between the Chinee's cooking and that of Widow Harris who loved to cook. Her late husband, dead at forty-two when his heart upped and stopped, had been a man of considerable substance – almost 230 pounds of it. Until his unfortunate passing there was no better way to measure the quality and quantity of Widow Harris's cooking than massively ponderous Robert Harris taking up two-thirds of a plankwalk when he went walking.

Eunice Harris was not a pretty woman. She was plain, direct and had been born with a minimal sense of humour although her sense of propriety was unequalled, at least in the Saddler's Wells settlement.

Sam Saddler commonly ate one meal a day at the rooming-house, supper. He and Doctor Morton were the only steady residents. There was an occasional travelling peddler, lawmen going north or south, itinerant preachers, but the only supper-time regulars after Marianne's departure were her father and her father's reason for sending her away.

As summer wore along the local leather man's reputation spread. His work was excellent, his prices were reasonable and he did something which was not common among those in his line of work; when he told someone their repairs or special orders would be finished by a certain time, that is when they could receive them.

One time he and Rattlesnake were sipping coffee at the leather works when Sam opened up enough to say he had been a saddle and harness man for nine years, but had given it up to do other things which paid better. He did not mention what the other things were and Rattlesnake did not ask.

Autumn arrived presaged by cooling nights, eventually frosty nights and the infrequent winds that seemed to come straight out of northerly ice fields.

That old pelter named Leonard who had identi-fied Alton Fisher the night of the botched bush-whacking, and two other old men, went to the foothills, downed and cut rounds from dead trees – green wood did not burn – and hauled it back to town in the ancient wagon one of the other old men owned pulled by a sway-backed ancient horse who had sunken places above each eye a man could put almost half a finger in.

Sam Saddler bought two cords of rounds and evenings before going to the rooming-house he would split rounds and stack the resulting firewood.

One cold, blustery night when Doc and Sam were dozing before the fireplace in the Widow Harris's parlour, old Leonard appeared at the door clutching an ancient hat in fingers blue from cold. He asked to speak to the leather man.

Widow Harris brought the old man to the parlour where Leonard said he would like to speak privately to the leather man. Widow Harris got a mug of hot coffee for Leonard and his gratitude was almost embarrassing.

He took Sam to the storeroom off the kitchen, emptied the coffee cup and said, 'I figured you'd ought to know. Me'n two other fellers was loadin' wood yestiddy when this feller on a sorrel horse come out of the trees. Needed a shave an' his hair was too long in back, but he was mannerly enough. He asked about the wood, the price, how hard it was to come by an' did we know if there was a feller called himself Sam Saddler down yonder in the town.'

Sam sat the old man on a flour barrel and left the door ajar between the kitchen which was almost too warm, and the storeroom. Leonard held the warm cup enclosed in both hands. He said, 'Feller didn't say his name. We didn't visit all that long. It was gettin' late an' we wanted to get back before dark.'

Sam asked what the rider looked like and Leonard answered without hesitation, 'Taller'n you, maybe forty or thereabouts, wore a buckskin ridin' coat and doeskin ropin' gloves. Nice-lookin' feller, had a pleasant way of talkin'. On the drive back we figured he was maybe your kinsman come to look you up.'

'Did he say he was coming here?'

'He – I'll tell you somethin' about him I figured later, after we got back; he talked real nice an' rode back into the trees without givin' us a chance to ask any questions.'

Sam leaned against a stair-stepped set of shelves

which were filled with bottles of put-up vegetables and meat. He sighed as he thanked Leonard for coming to see him, gave him a silver cartwheel and took him to the door where old Leonard seemed willing to talk but the leather man eased him out with a pat on the shoulder and closed the door.

Doc Morton was asleep in his parlour chair, the Widow Harris made clucking sounds. A God-fearing woman of almost sixty had her reputation to consider. She was not going to have Doc Morton sleeping all night in her parlour.

As Sam entered the parlour she asked if he would rouse Doc, which was no simple task and when Doc finally opened his eyes he widened them in a stare and moved to level himself upright and Sam suggested that Doc go home to bed down. He agreed by nodding, put on his hat, marched to the door, opened it and looked back straight at the leather man, stepped outside, closed the door and the Widow Harris made that clucking sound again. 'Acted like he'd seen a ghost. I suspect since Marianne left he's spendin' too much time at the saloon.'

Sam nodded absently, excused himself and went upstairs to his room. He got ready for bed but did not light a lamp, and with a high wind making the branches of a tree outside rake the siding, he lay awake a long time.

The following day the wind was gone but the air had a winy scent which derived from falling leaves, multi-coloured and plentiful.

The old men, bundled to the gullet with a horse blanket for the old pelter made of sew-together croaker sacks, sat hunched like gnomes on their

final trip to the uplands for wood. They passed
through about the time Chris Spartas swept out his
saloon. They waved and he waved back. As they
passed the leather works with its sheet where glass
had been, one old man chuckled as he said, 'Be
better if he boarded it up. He'll burn a cord of
wood tryin' to keep the shop warm.'

That was a reasonable prophesy, except that Sam
Saddler was not in his shop. Nor did he have
breakfast at the Chinee's eatery. He had been in
the saddle since before sun-up, with two wool shirts
layered under an old rangeman's sheep pelt riding
coat.

He reached timber long before the old men on
the wagon got close. After daybreak he sat his
saddle watching them. At the rate they travelled it
would be a good two hours before they reached
timber.

He dismounted, quartered until he found shod
horse sign, swore because last night's wind had
partially filled some of the tracks and began his
manhunt.

He depended as much on his thoroughbred
horse as he did on the tracks. A horse's vision is
excellent, its sense of smell is even better. No one
spent a bitterly cold night in the uplands without a
fire.

Sam was not fond of hiking, particularly in
country where the ground was rocky, the hills
steep, and the air cold.

Horsemen were not happy on foot. It had been
said the reason stockmen did not care for fishing
was because it could not be done from a saddle.

Sam was tracing along a sidehill following a game

trail when the horse snorted and sat back on the reins. Sam stopped. Ahead with a faint breeze ruffling it, was a red bandanna tied to a low limb of a scruffy pine tree.

Sam untied the bandanna, stuffed it into a coat pocket, looked in all directions and yelled.

'Why didn't you go all the way to the top?' was the reply. The voice was not loud and had a trace of amusement in it. 'Yell a little louder so those old gaffers with the wagon will hear you. Follow the trail straight ahead. I can see you. Sam, you look like you been eatin' regular. Keep comin'.'

4

Doubts

Old Leonard's description of the stranger was accurate. He was four or five inches taller than the leather man, wore a butter-coloured buckskin coat, and had an easy-going manner.

When he came from among some timber he was smiling. As Sam tethered his animal the stranger said, 'You find him?' and when Saddler shook his head the taller man asked another question. 'How long you been here?'

Sam finished with the horse and faced the taller man. 'Things like this take time. I know most folks down yonder, set up a harness shop in old Sam's building. Had a run in with some old sore-tail cowman named Watson—'

'An' you got no suspicion?'

'No.'

'Well,' the taller man said, 'I have. North-east of here there's a cow outfit owned by a man named Fedderson. You know him?'

'Nope.'

'I spent half a day with him. He remembers the shootin' real well. He was in town when it happened. He said a no-good son of a bitch who worked for the town blacksmith got into an argument with Uncle Ambrose at the saloon. How the killer left ahead of Uncle Ambrose an' how they met in the alley Fedderson had no idea, but Ambrose was higher'n a kite. He also said Uncle Ambrose had a reputation of hard drinkin'.'

'Did your cowman put a name to the blacksmith's helper?' Sam asked, and got a dry reply. 'Jake Smith.'

Sam considered the taller man. 'I know 'em all, mostly all of 'em in town, an' I never heard of any Jake Smith.'

'You know the blacksmith?' the tall man asked dryly.

'Yeah, to nod to.... When I get back I'll ask him about his helper.'

The tall man made another dry remark. 'If the son of a bitch is still in the country.'

Sam nodded and changed the subject of their conversation. 'How's Aunt Em?'

'You know Uncle Abe died?'

'Yes.'

'She makes out pretty well, but she misses him. An' you.'

'Did she show you the letters I wrote?'

'That's how I knew where you were. Sam, it bothered her when Ambrose got killed.'

Sam could hear a wagon and cut this meeting short. 'You goin' to camp out or come into town?' he asked, and the tall man considered his answer before giving it. 'For what we're goin' to do it might be better if I stayed clear of the town. I got my army heliograph mirror. You watch for it.'

Sam nodded as he untied his thoroughbred horse. After he had swung into the saddle the taller man said, 'How old is he now?'

Sam patted the thoroughbred's neck as he replied. 'Eight.'

'In his prime. You raced him lately?'

'No, an' I don't expect to. Not here. Not until we get things settled, an' maybe not even then.'

The last thing Sam said as he was reining around to travel westerly so he wouldn't encounter the old woodcutters, was that if the tall man needed to reach him, he could do it by coming down the back alley to the harness shop, otherwise he boarded at the Widow Harris's place. Anyone could tell him where that was.

Sam did not reach town until early evening. He'd had to make an extended sashay to avoid Leonard and his partners, and by the time he was nearing the southward roadway the sun was teetering on some distant sawtooth rims.

Rattlesnake was not around – probably at supper at the Chinee's eatery – so Sam cared for his horse himself, forked feed and filled the small grain box.

He stood a long time in thickening shadows. His cousin had been clearly annoyed that Sam hadn't accomplished more for the length of time he'd been in Saddler's Wells. And he had no excuse.

He went along to the boarding-house, nodded to Widow Harris and cleaned up out back before entering the dining-room to be fed. This particular evening Doc Morton was absent and three travelling salesmen were at the table.

Conversation was minimal. Sam was not a man who made conversation for the sake of it, and evidently the travelling peddlers were the same kind of men.

When he was ready to go upstairs to his room Widow Harris nailed him. She was worried about Doc. In a low voice she told Sam if Doc was at the saloon ... 'He's had heart trouble for years, you know.'

Sam hadn't known any such thing but he said he'd find Doc and bring him back, to which the widow stated flatly that Sam was to take Doc to his own residence and bed him down there. She did not want folks seeing a staggering Doctor Morton entering her house at night.

Sam was tired. He'd been a-horseback all day and the amount of supper he'd put away added to his loggy feeling. He nevertheless left the house heading to Spartas's water-hole.

It was cold with a lively little wind blowing. Most stores were not only dark but had their steel shutters closed and latched from the inside.

Before Sam entered the saloon he could hear loud voices, two in particular, who seemed to be arguing fiercely. When he pushed inside where lamplight temporarily blinded him he heard Chris explaining loudly that he allowed no fighting in his establishment. If the arguers wanted to settle things they should go out into the road.

One of the arguers was Rattlesnake Rowe who waved his bandaged arm as he tried to out-shout the other man, who was shorter, grey as a badger and clearly a rangeman. He was armed, Rattlesnake was not.

Chris used an ash spoke from below the counter to strike the bar for silence. When the profanity diminished the Greek pointed to the spindle doors with his spoke and said, 'Out! Both of you – out!'

The shorter, bull-built man with the grey thatch started to protest, which was a mistake. Spartas started toward the end of the bar waving his ash spoke.

Rattlesnake saw Sam in the doorway. 'This mongrel bastard said I—'

'*Out*,' the Greek exclaimed loudly raising his ash spoke in a threatening way. 'Smith, don't you never come into my saloon again! You was troublesome when you worked in town. *Out or I'll bust your damned skull!*'

The stocky man glared as he retreated in the direction of the doors. He was looking over his shoulder and bumped into the leather man, who caught Smith by the arm and shoved him away. Smith's fury was blind. When someone grabbed him he tore clear and swung a rock-hard right fist. Sam was rocked by the blow. Smith faced him in the doorway snarling and poised to strike again.

Sam tried to paw the enraged man away, but Smith bore ahead. His second blow caught the leather man high and to the left. Again Sam was staggered, but when he recovered he sidestepped. When the third blow came it missed and Sam met the angry rangeman coming back around.

The blow sounded like the distant report of a pistol. The rangeman went down on his face.

Chris came up with his spoke poised. Sam pointed a finger and the Greek hesitated. The saloon was crowded, but for ten seconds a falling pin would have sounded loud.

Rattlesnake came over, looked down, looked up, and said, 'That was as handy a piece of footwork as I've seen in ages.'

Chris ignored everything but the unconscious man on the floor. 'Drag the son of a bitch out of here. Even when he worked in town he picked fights. Drag him out of here!'

No one moved to comply with the irate Greek's order, but Rattlesnake spoke to Sam. 'Chris is right. When he worked for Lacy he was ornery. Lacy said he was a good forge man, an' after he left the smithy to ride for that old man we backed down the other day—'

Sam interrupted. 'What's his name, Rattlesnake?'

'Jake Smith.'

'He worked for the blacksmith?'

'Yes. Until he quit to work for old man Watson as a rider.'

Sam said, 'Lend a hand, Rattlesnake – your good one. Let's drag him outside.'

As the door shuddered closed behind Rattlesnake, Sam and their inert companion, Chris stamped back behind his bar, black eyes still smouldering, put away his 'peacemaker', and loudly proclaimed that if Jake Smith ever entered his saloon again he'd use the sawn-off shotgun, also kept on the shelf below the bar.

Because the Greek's ire did not dissipate most of his customers paid up and left, which Spartas blamed on the blacksmith's helper turned range rider, which was only partly right. No one felt comfortable in a saloon where the proprietor glared and snarled as he set up drinks.

Sam and Rattlesnake, for lack of a better place, half dragged, half carried their feebly struggling companion down to the livery barn.

Rattlesnake suggested whiskey to clear Smith's cobwebs. Sam took a bucket to the trough out back, returned and flung its contents on Jake Smith, who staggered backwards until his knees struck the edge of the bench outside the harness room, and sat down making noises like a fish out of water.

Rattlesnake recited instances of Jake Smith's bad actions in town. Everyone except the blacksmith was relieved when Smith quit the smithy and hired on with the cowman named Watson.

It was late; only Spartas's lights still burned. There was an ankle-high gusty little cold wind stirring dust the full length of Main Street, and eventually Rattlesnake's arm began bothering him so he left Sam with the soggy, venomous-eyed Watson rider. Sam remembered seeing Smith among Watson's men. In fact it had been Smith who would have contested where Sam and Spartas tied their horses.

Smith looked like a drowned rat. He shivered and looked squarely at Sam as he said, 'I know you. You braced old man Watson in his yard – somethin' to do with a broke winder.'

Sam replied dryly, 'Not exactly about the busted window. Watson and Fisher ambushed Rowe, the feller who helped drag you down here.'

Smith used a soggy handkerchief to mop his face and tucked it away before speaking again. 'Mister, if Al Fisher figured to ambush somebody, believe me they'd be dead.'

'It was close,' Sam acknowledged, and changed the subject. 'Tell me about your fight with Ambrose in the alley out back of the livery barn.'

Smith's muddy gaze was fixed on the leather man. 'Who told you it was me out there with Ambrose?'

'That don't matter. It was you. Him'n you got into it at the saloon an' he was shot to death directly after the pair of you left.'

'That don't prove nothin'. When Ambrose was drinkin' – which was most of the time – he was troublesome. Ask around; folks'll tell you.'

Sam considered the mean-faced, soaking wet man without blinking. 'Who else would have shot him?' he asked.

Smith's eyes narrowed. 'Off hand I could name half a dozen. Ambrose was trouble four ways from the middle. Even when he was comin' off a drunk he was disagreeable-mean an' mouthy.'

Sam sighed. 'Once more,' he said. 'Why did you shoot him?'

Smith mimicked Sam. 'One more time, who said I shot him?'

Sam backhanded Smith across the face. When Smith recovered he put a hand to his mouth. There was a tiny trickle of blood. He started to arise and Sam punched him back down. Smith's next words were venomous. 'I'll tell you. We dang near got into a fight at the saloon. That damned Greek run us both out. You seen how crazy he acts with that wagon spoke. We left. Ambrose almost fell off the duckboards. I caught his arm. Mister, he was fallin'-down drunk. He didn't even know who I was. I told him I didn't fight women, babies or drunks, to go somewhere'n sleep it off, an' the next day if he was willin' I'd meet him in the middle of the road.'

Sam listened briefly to a dog barking somewhere near the upper end of town. When he returned his gaze to Jake Smith he had a forming doubt. Smith had sounded truthful, defiantly so. He asked Smith if he knew a stockman named Fedderson and Smith made a sour face. 'I know him. So does Lacy. He's one of them sons of bitches that can't shoe a horse but stands lookin' over your shoulder tellin' you how to do it. What about him?'

Sam ignored the question to ask one of his own. 'Who else was in the alley?'

Smith groaned. 'I wasn't in the damned alley so how could I tell you that!'

'What did you an' Ambrose get into a fight about at the saloon?'

'A horse. I said it was six years old. Ambrose said it was nine. Mister, I mouthed that horse. It was six.'

'And you called him a liar?'

Smith shifted slightly on the bench before replying. 'What would you do in a saloon full of men when someone ups an' the same as calls you a liar?'

'An' you lit into him,' said Sam.

Smith groaned again. 'I told you he was fallin'-down drunk. He couldn't even find his holster. Spartas run us out when we got to yellin' at each other. The last I seen of him he was leanin' on the tie-rack.'

'You didn't follow him to the alley?'

'Gawddammit no!'

Sam asked a question which had its source in the cowman named Fedderson. 'Why would anyone say they saw you shoot Ambrose if you didn't?'

'How'n hell would I know!'

'They tell me you got a bad reputation.'

Smith shrugged that off. 'I done my share of fightin' if that's what you mean.' Smith briefly brightened. 'Ask Walt Lacy. I worked for him close to three years.'

'You'n him got along, did you?'

Again Smith hung fire before replying. 'We had our differences. You never had disagreements with outfits you worked for?'

'How come you to hire on with Mister Watson?'

'Because one of his riders quit, an' with him makin' a gather he needed another man.'

'He hired you?'

'Naw. Al Fisher did.' Smith seemed about to add more but in the end he didn't.

'You goin' north with Watson?'

'Figure to. That's what he hired me for, an' besides I'm sick of Saddler's Wells.'

Smith groped in a shirt pocket, brought forth a soggy plug of Mule Shoe which he regarded with obvious disgust and tossed it away. He looked enquiringly at Sam, who shook his head. Sam did not chew tobacco.

Smith's lower lip was swollen but the bleeding had stopped. At his best he was not a tidy individual but now, with water soaking the ground at his feet, he looked like something a pup might drag home from a tanyard.

He abruptly said something that made the leather man's eyes narrow. 'When you'n the liveryman come out to the cow camp....'

'Go on.'

'You recollect a rider sayin' somethin' to Mister Watson before he give you money for your winder?'

Sam nodded.

'His name's Bud Foster. What he told the old man was that he remembered you'n your cousin from Texas. He told the old man you cleaned out a gamblin' hall down there full of rangemen, killed one and shot up three others. He told the old man you'n your cousin was called the fastest an' deadliest gunmen in all of West Texas.' Smith looked hard at Sam. 'Is that true?'

Sam inclined his head and faintly smiled.

'I'd like to hear how you done it,' Smith said, and Sam told him to stand up, which Smith did while Sam went over him for maybe a boot knife or a hideout belly gun. He found nothing and Smith sneered, 'Them things is for fellers that drink water.'

Sam pushed Smith back down on the bench. 'You'n me are goin' to take a horseback ride.'

'Now, for Chris'sake, in the middle of the damned night? What for?'

'I want to talk to Mister Fedderson with you along.'

Smith stared without saying a word until he had wagged his head. 'He said he was in the alley an' saw me shoot Ambrose? What do you think he'll say again? The same damned lie.'

'Maybe, but I want to know why he said it. How well do you know him?'

'I told you; he's a big fat lump of lard, thinks he knows it all.'

'But why would he say he saw you kill Ambrose?'

'How in hell would I know? But I can tell you the gospel truth: I didn't dog Ambrose to the alley and shoot him.'

Sam said, 'Don't move,' and led his horse out to be rigged for riding. Smith, with all his troubles, admired the thoroughbred and said so as Sam told him to walk in the middle of the road up to the tie-rack out front of the saloon, which was dark now.

They left town at a dead walk. Sam had to rely on Smith to lead the way. It was a fair distance, they were still riding when half of a red sun showed above the horizon. Smith cursed the cold even though he had shrugged into the rider's coat rolled and tied behind his cantle. Its warmth did not offset the cold water he'd been drenched with. Some miles up the northerly roadway where Smith reined north-easterly, Smith suddenly said, 'You see that flash of light?'

Sam looked up-country without answering, was still looking up there when two more flashes came, very brief and very bright.

Smith said, 'Soldiers. What'll they be doin' up in them mountains?'

Sam switched his attention to the country ahead, which had its share of buckbrush and manzanita but which also had clumps of buffalo grass. He asked Smith how large an outfit Fedderson had and got a curt reply. 'Runs maybe four, five hunnert cows.'

'How many hired riders?'

'Only him an' his son. His wife up an' died last year. Folks in town said they expected him to sell out.'

'How well do you know him?'

'Passable well. Me'n Walt Lacy shod some harness horses for him an' now'n then a ridin' horse. He's one of them men who don't put on new shoes until a horse's feet are six, eight inches long, or if they cast a wore out shoe an' get tender. I don't like the son of a bitch. Neither did Walt Lacy, but when you're runnin' a smithy you got to take what comes along.' Smith paused, then also said, 'Folks in town know Fedderson.'

'What does that mean?'

'They don't like him.'

'Why?'

Smith looked at Sam. 'I already as good as told you. He's a penny-pinchin', poker-faced, sly son of a bitch who knows it all an' ain't bashful about lettin' you know it.'

When they topped out over a long landswell and Sam saw buildings about a mile ahead, Smith said, 'That's it. There's smoke risin' from the kitchen stove pipe. Maybe we can get somethin' to eat.'

Sam studied the set of buildings without speaking. Fedderson's outbuildings seemed not to have been cared for since being built. The corral stringers had been patched with different sized logs and the main house had a sagging roofline and a broken window someone had nailed boards across.

5

Emory's Tale

A fair distance before they reached the yard with
its unkempt old trees, Sam saw a gangling youth
appear on the porch, remain still for a few
moments then duck back inside.

When next he appeared there was a thick,
greying man with several chins and a formidable
paunch with him. They remained in place until
Sam and his companion reached the tie-rack in
front of the barn, then the large, heavy man came
down off the porch and walked ponderously
toward the newcomers standing with their horses.

When the fat man got a good look at Sam's
companion his step momentarily faltered. When
he was close enough he ignored Sam and boomed a
hearty, patently false greeting, and Smith replied
in the same way, except that he jerked his thumb in
Sam's direction as he said, 'This gent would like
words with you, Mister Fedderson.'

The fat man shoved out a massive and pulpy

hand which Sam pumped once and released as he said, 'My name's Sam Saddler. I got the harness works in town.'

The fat man nodded. To Sam's knowledge he had never been in the shop, but that wasn't necessary in a small town. Fedderson knew where the shop was.

He introduced his gangling son first. 'This here is my boy, Henry. Folks call him Hank.'

Sam gripped the lanky youth's hand and released it. Henry Fedderson had deep-set eyes and a direct gaze. He did not resemble his father. He was lean and almost solemn.

The fat man said, 'I'm Moses Fedderson. Moe for short.' Moe Fedderson put a long, steady look at Smith. 'Somethin' I can do for you gents?' Fedderson's gaze remained fixed on Smith as he spoke.

Sam answered quietly. 'The way I heard it you said you saw Mister Smith shoot my pa, Ambrose, in the alley behind the livery barn.'

Fedderson's brown eyes did not leave Smith's face when he replied to Sam. 'That's what I seen.'

Smith growled an obscenity and tilted to charge, fists knotted. Sam had no time to stop Smith but the gangling youth did. He drew and cocked his six-gun. For five seconds all four men seemed to have taken root. Sam quietly told Hank Fedderson to put up his gun, which the youth did not do until his father also told him to.

Sam was surprised at the speed of the youth's draw. Fedderson looked straight at Sam when next he spoke. 'I was at the barn an' had to pee so I went out into the alley. I didn't notice Ambrose and Jake until one or the other of 'em called the other one a no-good lyin' bastard. There was one gunshot. Ambrose went down. Smith's back was to me until he faced toward the runway, then I seen him plain as day.'

Sam asked if Fedderson was the only man in the alley except for Smith and Ambrose. Fedderson slowly nodded. 'I didn't know it until the gunshot sounded. There was someone across the alley near some corrals. He was facin' Ambrose. After the gunshot he disappeared. There wasn't much of a moon that night.'

Sam asked if the fat man could identify the third man and got a head shake. 'The gunshot blinded me for a time, an' whoever he was he was gone when I looked for him.'

Sam faced Jake Smith, who was red to the hairline with his glaring stare fixed on the fat man. Smith spoke through clenched teeth.

'He's lyin' for all he's worth. He never saw me in the alley because I wasn't out there.'

Sam might have agreed, for a fact someone was lying and he had to grudgingly admit Moe Fedderson sounded believable, but then so had Jake Smith.

He had another question for Fedderson. 'You knew Ambrose pretty well, did you?'

Fedderson shrugged massive shoulders. 'Everyone knew him. Couldn't not know him. He wasn't a feller who worked at bein' liked. Him'n Jake got into it the night Ambrose got shot. Ask anyone who was in the saloon that night.' Fedderson's gaze drifted back to Smith. 'Ambrose was obnoxious but he couldn't find his behind with both hands when he'd been drinkin', and the night he was killed he was that drunk, mister. Killin' anyone the shape Ambrose was in that night would be like takin' candy from a baby.'

Jake's lips were sucked flat, his glare was murderous. When Fedderson paused for air Smith spoke very clearly. 'You lyin' son of a bitch! Every danged thing you just said is a damned lie from start to finish an' you know it.'

The fat man did not act particularly upset. Behind and to one side of him his gangling son stared at Jake Smith from an expressionless face.

Sam knew that look and that stance. He asked the father if the son had been in town with him the night of the killing.

Fedderson glanced briefly at his tight-wound son before answering. 'No. We had three heifers fixin' to calve. Hank stayed home to mind them.'

'So you went to town alone,' Sam said, and Fedderson's gaze did not waver when he nodded.

Jake Smith held clenched fists at his side. He was having a difficult time of it. Sam jerked his head for Smith to get astride, which Smith did. The last thing the leather man did was brush his hatbrim in Moe Fedderson's direction before he straightened around to follow Jake Smith from the yard.

Father and son did not move until their visitors were small in the distance, then Moe told his son to put the harness mare in the buggy shafts, that they'd go to town.

Hank never disobeyed, nor did he this time. By the time he had the buggy ready his father came from the house and Moe Fedderson was not smiling.

On the return ride Jake turned the air blue with fiercely profane denunciations of both Feddersons. He said if he could meet Moe Fedderson man-to-man he'd gut shoot him.

Sam looked around. 'That boy's your worry, more'n the fat man.'

Jake's smouldering anger included Sam Saddler when he turned and said, 'Tell me why he lied in his teeth with me standin' right there?'

That is what had been troubling Sam. One of them was a bald-faced liar and both were world-class liars.

'Why?' Jake demanded in a snarl.

Sam's reply was quietly given. 'That's what I'm havin' trouble with. Ambrose had nothin'. Why would someone kill him?'

'I told you,' Jake growled. 'He was a cantan-kerous, no-good drunk with a nasty way of actin'. Men like him have been killed every place I've ever been just because they rub folks the wrong way.'

'A fallin'-down drunk?'

'Sure. There's always some thin-skinned son of a bitch who takes things personal, an' Ambrose had a bad mouth, worse when he was drunk.'

Sam considered the unkempt, mean-eyed man he was riding with. Jake Smith was probably just about anything someone had to say about him, but what he had just said offered the leather man an unintended view of Jake Smith. Whatever else he was, Jake was not thin-skinned.

When they reached town Rattlesnake was in the runway with a rake. He dropped the rake to take their horses. While he was doing this he said Frank Watson and his rangeboss were in town looking for

Jake. Smith started to retrieve the reins from
Rattlesnake when Sam told the liveryman to stall
Jake's animal, feed it, water it and Jake would be
along for it in an hour or so.

Jake appeared more puzzled than angry. Sam
bumped him into moving and cross the road on a
diagonal course to the Chinee's café.

When Jake smelled food his demeanour
changed. He had been hungry before making the
ride to the Fedderson place, when he smelled
cooking he sank down at the counter, thumbed
back his hat and yelled for the proprietor to bring
coffee first, then a double order of whatever
smelled good.

Jake ate, his manner detached, puzzlement
noticeable in his expression. When they had been
fed Jake wanted to go to the emporium for a fresh
plug of Mule Shoe. Sam went along. When they
entered the store the high-strung, eternally
distrustful proprietor stood staring. When Jake put
coins atop the counter for his plug, Carlyle said,
'Where you been? Mister Watson's been lookin'
high an' low for you. He was in town until about an
hour ago.'

Jake scowled. 'Mule Shoe.'

Carlyle got one plug from the box, scooped up
the coins and stared at Sam, who smiled and
accompanied Jake back to the roadway where Jake
gnawed off his first cud in many hours, tucked it
into his cheek and said, 'Fedderson lied; everything
he said was a lie.'

Sam said the same thing Jake had said on the
ride to town. 'Why?'

Jake turned aside to spray amber, shifted the cud

and finally answered. 'I don't know, but for a fact a man don't lie like Fedderson did without a reason.' Jake considered the distance to the livery barn and the distance to the saloon. The latter distance was closer. He told Sam he'd stand the first round and waited for Sam to agree. Instead the leather man said, 'Go on back to Watson's camp. When you tell 'em where you been an' who you was with, they might not chew on you for bein' gone so long.'

Jake's brows contracted a little. 'Are you tryin' to tell me somethin'?'

Sam smiled. 'If I wanted to tell you somethin' I'd come straight out with it.'

Jake walked southward in the direction of the livery barn. Twice he paused to look over his shoulder. Each time Sam raised a hand in a salute. Later he went to his shop, entered from the alley and was in the process of kicking out of his boots, shedding his hat and gun belt when a noise out front caught his attention. He went out there gun in hand and his cousin looked up from a bench and smiled. 'Have you forgot our signal? Three flashes an' I'm comin' to see you.'

Sam went behind the counter to sit on a stool at the cutting table. He told his cousin about the visit with Moses Fedderson and the taller man was quiet for a spell before saying, 'I didn't tell you, but the longer I visited with him the less I liked him.' The taller man arose from the wall bench, leaned on the counter and spoke again. 'I had the smith reshoe my horse. You know him?'

'Not real well.'

'Well, you should because don't nothin' happen around here he either don't know about or got an opinion about. We visited for quite a spell. He told me his idea about somethin' that's bothered me for some time. Why would anyone want Uncle Ambrose dead?'

'From what I've heard,' Sam retorted, 'he had a foul disposition an' when he'd been drinkin' it got worse.'

The taller man gazed pensively at Sam Saddler. 'The blacksmith told me an interestin' story. The squinty-eyed weasel who runs the general store used Uncle Ambrose to haul freight for him. This was some time before the feller they call Rattlesnake started up his livery, tradin' an' freightin' business.'

Sam shifted position. His cousin had always been a drawling, long-winded person. 'Get on with it,' he said.

The smiling taller man nodded. 'You know the storekeeper?'

'Art Carlyle? Everybody knows him.'

'Uncle Ambrose did, accordin' to Mister Lacy. He told me him'n Uncle Ambrose was close friends. He told me he never believed that feller who used to be his forge man killed Uncle Ambrose. But he said that's what folks believe, and it could cost him his livin' to say otherwise.'

Sam went around the counter to a more comfortable seat and sat down. He sat stone-faced listening to his cousin, and in the back of his mind he had just found some justification for his doubts. He asked his cousin who the blacksmith thought had killed Ambrose, and got a saturnine look and head wag. 'He said he could guess but that wouldn't be good enough. I said go ahead, guess, an' he asked me what my interest was.'

'An' you told him the truth?'

The taller man looked pained. 'Aunt Em didn't raise no idiots. I lied. My interest, I told him, was simply that of someone listenin' to a good spinner of yarns.' The taller man smiled. 'Folks like to be cottoned to. The blacksmith did. He told me about a cowman, one of them seasonal ones, who peed through the same knothole as this storekeeper – whose name is Watson. He said Uncle Ambrose would go north an' return with a loaded wagon covered with wagon canvas.' The tall man paused. He clearly enjoyed long-winded recitations.

Sam waited, not patiently but silently.

'Mister Lacy told me Uncle Ambrose hauled guns and ammunition, and Mister Watson's riders did the out-ridin' until Ambrose got close to here then they left an' Uncle Ambrose put the wagon in the big storage shed behind the emporium.'

'And …?'

'That's all the blacksmith knew, but he figured someone come along, most likely at night, and drove the wagon away.'

'Drove it where?'

The taller man looked briefly annoyed. 'He didn't know. I just told you, it was done on the sly.'

'An' you're sayin' Ambrose got killed because he knew he was haulin' guns?'

'No. He said Uncle Ambrose was killed because he got to drinkin' and when he was smoked up he shot off his mouth.'

Sam went back by the cutting table and reperched on the stool. He said, 'There's no law against haulin' guns,' and his cousin agreed. 'Sure not. Unless you're peddlin' 'em to tomahawks or

Mex border jumpers, then the army don't like it.' The taller man changed position against the counter. 'Seems to me that before we find Uncle Ambrose's killer, we got to know where them guns went.'

'How do we find that out?'

The taller man shifted against the counter again. 'I'd guess from the storekeeper, or maybe other folks who knew as much as the blacksmith knew. How about Moses Fedderson? If he would lie through his teeth about the killin', I wonder why, unless he was maybe paid to lie, an' who would pay him? How well you know Mister Watson?'

Sam delayed his reply. He was havin' difficulty placing old Watson in the story his cousin had related. Not because he did not believe Watson would get involved in something like illegal gun-running, but because Watson had impressed him as a full-time cowman, one whose income was adequate without partnering up with anyone dealing in contraband.

On the other hand old Watson had not impressed Sam favourably. He was mean and cantankerous. A man like that might enjoy gun-running.

His cousin repeated the question. 'How well do you know Watson?'

'As well as I want to. I've had a couple of run-ins with him. Why?'

'Seems to me, Sam, someone's got to chum up with him.'

Sam snorted. 'Only thing I can imagine that old bastard'd chum up with is maybe a rattler or a gila monster.'

Sam arose and paced the room. Beyond the sheet covering the window hole could be heard men calling to one another, shod animals using the roadway, and some not-too-distant chickens.

When he turned to regard the taller man he said, 'Emory, about the blacksmith ... I never heard anythin' about Ambrose haulin' freight.'

The taller man briefly pondered before dryly saying, 'He also told me about how you arrived in town – four dead Messicans an' one runnin' for his life. Is that true, Sam?'

'There's no connection.'

'Don't have to be. What I'm sayin' is that why would the blacksmith make up a tale that could get him killed out of the whole cloth?'

Sam eyed his cousin. 'True or not he could get himself killed anyway, if his version got around. An' for all we know it maybe already has.'

Emory Saddler shrugged. 'If I'm not the first one his conscience made him let his hair down to, he'd already be dead. He was stone sober, Sam. My guess is that it's been buildin' up in him for a long time. Him an' Uncle Ambrose was close friends.' The tall man twisted on the counter to face Sam. 'You stay in town. On my way back to the mountains I'll look up Mister Fedderson an' have a talk with him. He might turn out to be real helpful.'

Sam reached inside his shirt to briefly scratch. 'Emory, if you overhaul him enough so he breaks down, it'll get to Watson an' Carlyle by morning.'

Emory Saddler straightened up off the counter and smiled. He was five or six years older than Sam. 'That don't amount to much of a problem,' he said, and went back through the lean-to, let himself out of the shop, made sure the alley was empty and went to where his tethered horse was dozing.

Sam returned to the bench, sat down and digested what had been said and came to the conclusion that his cousin was right about one thing: to get at the bottom of what he was convinced had been a murder, someone had to provide information, and since he did not believe Jake Smith had committed the murder, Moses Fedderson was the only person he knew of who knew enough to lie like a trooper.

Arthur Carlyle came over to somewhat breathlessly say Sam's replacement glass window had arrived from up north. He also said this was the fastest he'd ever received freight.

Sam eyed the nervous man whose movements were bird-like, and said he'd look up the town carpenter and come after the window in the morning, to which Carlyle cleared his throat and drummed lightly on the counter. 'Includin' freight,' he said, 'the charges is eight an' a half dollars. I'm sorry, Sam, but I got no control over what freighters charge. It's highway robbery but years back when I hauled my own freight a freighter wouldn't be able to look a man in the face an' charge what they ask for nowadays. If you need Farrel the carpenter, I saw him enter the saloon when I come over here.'

After the wiry storekeeper had departed Sam returned briefly to the bench before going after the carpenter. Twice in the same day he'd been told Carlyle used to do his own freighting. It didn't have to prove anything. On the other hand it could very well prove something.

By the time he got over to the saloon the carpenter had returned to his small, littered shop near the north end of town, just short of the tanyard. When Sam arrived up there the carpenter, a large, bony individual with pale-blue eyes and a thatch which had once been blond and was now grey-blond, was eating an apple. He hastily pitched the core aside, dried both hands on his coveralls and listened when Sam mentioned the window.

The carpenter would do the job first thing after breakfast in the morning.

Sam returned to his shop, sat a while in thought before heading for the Chinee's eatery, and from there visited the saloon where the Greek complimented him on having a new glass window.

Sam stared; the only way to prevent something from becoming common knowledge in Saddler's Wells was to tell it first.

6

A Palaver

Warnings commonly arrive intuitively, by word of mouth or even by simple expectations or suspicions, but the warning Sam Saddler got the morning after his cousin's visit was the kind that stopped his breathing after opening the alleyway door of his shop.

Jake Smith had been propped up across the alley facing Sam's rear doorway. There was a puckered, bluish swollen place not quite in the centre of his forehead. The eyes were dry with both lids half closed.

Sam crossed the alley and leaned. There was no trace of powder burns; Smith had been shot at a distance. Bushwhacked sure as hell.

Sam did not visit the eatery, he saddled the thoroughbred and rode due north. It was still early and although the sun was well up the morning was chilly.

He did not worry about finding his cousin,

Emory would have clear vision for miles of southward country. He would see a solitary rider, from a great distance but could not make a sure identification until Sam was less than a mile distant. There was only one horse with the bearing of Sam's thoroughbred.

Emory left camp and went afoot part way down-slope and when Sam arrived the taller man took a long look at the leather man's face and said, 'What happened?'

Sam offered no customary greeting. He told the tall man about Jake Smith as he led his horse in the direction of his cousin's camp where there was one of those rare small meadows of emerald green grass where he hobbled the thoroughbred.

The tall man's camp was a study in frugality. There was a fire ring of rocks, a small pot and a larger dry pan. There was also a neat pile of dry wood twigs and a canteen hanging from a tree. Emory's riding gear was upended with the blanket sweat-side up. He sank to the ground, eyed Sam and said, 'I went by Fedderson's place but he wasn't there. Neither was the lad nor his buggy.'

Sam seemed not to have heard. 'I expect it was my fault for takin' Smith to the Fedderson place with me. Somebody figured Smith was helpin' me. But I wanted 'em face to face.'

'When did you see him last?'

'When he was leavin' town to go out to the Watson camp.'

Emory scratched inside his shirt. 'I saw dust yesterday where men was makin' a gather.'

Sam nodded. 'Watson. He comes south for grass until it's gone then trails back up north. That's likely what you saw, a Watson gather.'

The taller man squinted. 'Watson. The name crops up, don't it?'

Sam picked up a twig and made squiggly marks in the dust as he answered. 'We need Fedderson.'

Emory watched the squiggle marks being made when he replied, 'I'll get him. Come back tonight. I'll have him here.'

Sam raised his eyes. He knew his cousin as well as anyone did, but getting Fedderson might not be as easy as finding him. If whoever shot Jake Smith did it because he knew Sam and Jake had been together, had possibly learned about it from Fedderson, to Sam's knowledge the only person who could inform about that visit.

He said, 'If Fedderson got spooked you might have a hard time finding him, an' if you do more'n likely he won't be alone.'

Emory smiled. 'Me'n Mister Fedderson got real friendly, an' he don't know you'n me even know each other. Go on back and if I find him watch for the heliograph about supper time.'

Sam went after his horse, rigged it, led it back where his cousin was sitting and said, 'If you can't find Fedderson we got one left, the storekeeper.'

The taller man nodded, waited until Sam was astride and said, 'If there is a signal about sunset, ride on up.'

Sam nodded and rode back down-slope, angled easterly to the roadway and reached town with the sun behind his right shoulder.

Rattlesnake was dozing on a kicked-back chair in his runway when the leather man rode in, swung off and yanked the latigo free. Rattlesnake opened his eyes, watched then got to his feet to take the horse. 'Some lads playin' in the alley behind your shop found Jake Smith dead with a bullet hole in him.' If this was said to surprise Sam, it failed to do so. As he watched Rattlesnake leading the horse to water he spoke over his shoulder. 'Ike Farrel put your new winder in.'

Sam went northward and sure enough, the shot-out window had been replaced. Across the road someone called to him. 'Dollar be all right?'

Sam turned. He and the carpenter met in the middle of the road where Sam handed over the silver cartwheel. As he accepted it the carpenter said, 'If you've been gone most of the day maybe you didn't know Jake Smith was propped up across the alley with a bullet hole in him.'

Again, if Sam was supposed to act surprised, he wasn't. He thanked the carpenter, returned to his shop, went inside, made a routine inspection until he was satisfied no one had been in the shop during his absence, and was examining the fit of the new window when he saw Hank Fedderson enter the general store. He seemed to have been alone.

Sam crossed the road and was lingering in front of the saloon when Moses Fedderson's son emerged carrying a sack. The lad saw Sam and quickly looked away. He had a large, pudding-footed horse at the tie-rack and was making the sack secure behind the cantle when Sam spoke behind him. The lad whirled. Sam said, 'Your pa come in with you?'

'No. We're missin' some cows. He went lookin' for 'em.'

'Care to eat supper with me?' Sam asked, and got a swiftly spoken nervous refusal. 'I got to get back.'

Sam waited until the lad was astride before speaking again. 'That feller who rode out with me yesterday to see your pa: someone shot him an' left him propped across the alley from my shop.'

Hank Fedderson had obviously already heard about that. As he evened up the reins he said, 'I got to get back,' and whirled his mount to lope northward. His face had been white to the hairline.

Rattlesnake came along, on his way to the eatery. He watched young Fedderson and said, 'I'll tell you somethin' about that lad: he spends his free time practisin' with guns.'

Sam nodded. 'You do a lot of foolish things when you're young. The trouble with gettin' good with guns is that someday, someone'll come along who is better.'

They entered the café together, sat at the counter, called their orders and while waiting Rattlesnake said, 'There's talk about Jake. Why did someone go to all the effort of luggin' his carcass back to town an' proppin' it across from your back door?'

Sam leaned back as the caféman appeared with two platters. 'Looks good,' he told the caféman. Beside him Rattlesnake hadn't finished with the Jake Smith topic. He said, 'You'n Jake left town together yestiddy mornin'.'

Sam went to work on his meal without commenting. If Rattlesnake had been a tactful individual he'd also have gone to eating. With knife and fork in hand he said, 'Don't take me wrong but there's talk you'n Jake may have locked horns.'

Sam put down his eating utensils and turned. 'If I'd have shot the son of a bitch would I have propped him across the alley from my shop?'

Rattlesnake reddened and attacked his meal. Not another word was said between them until they were outside with dusk approaching and Sam peering northward. Rattlesnake had one more comment to make. 'When Doc come for the body with his wagon, he did what he always does, puts everythin' from a corpse into a big envelope.'

Sam faced back around, waiting.

'There was a paper stuck in Jake's shirt pocket. It said, "You got twenty-four hours".'

Sam faced his companion. 'He should have taken that advice.'

'Who?'

'Jake. Who else?'

Rattlesnake ruminated briefly before nodding and turning in the direction of his barn.

Sam stood a while watching northward. The sun was setting, dusk was close. His cousin could not signal without sunlight. He was still standing there when Doctor Morton came along on his way to the eatery. He paused, frowned and said, 'You heard about Jake Smith?'

Sam nodded.

'He had a scrap of paper stuffed in a shirt pocket.'

'I heard about that too. Doc, Jake made a mistake; he went ridin' with me yestiddy.'

Morton studied Sam from shrewd eyes. 'Except that I'm never goin' ridin' with you – there's somethin' goin' on folks don't understand.'

Sam was facing northerly. He was looking over

Doc's shoulder when he saw the flash, two flashes
in fact, not very bright but unmistakable. He said,
'Doc, tell your daughter I hope she's havin' a good
visit.'

Sam crossed the road leaving Doctor Morton
peering after him. Doc finally shook his head and
continued on toward the eatery.

Rattlesnake was dunging out stalls when Sam
arrived, got his thoroughbred, bridled and saddled
it without speaking and Rattlesnake leaned on the
handle of his four-tined fork watching. Only when
Sam led the horse toward the roadway before
mounting did Rattlesnake move, then all he did
was push his wheelbarrow to the next stall to be
dunged out. He told the horse he tied outside, his
friend the leather man was up to his hocks in
something, sure as the Good Lord had made sour
apples.

For Sam the cool evening provided a blessing.
He did not ordinarily ride the thoroughbred out of
a lope, but this time as he headed for timbered
country he let the horse have its head and being a
critter born and raised to run, who enjoyed
freedom after being stalled, the big horse covered
most of the distance in record time.

When Sam slackened off he was near the uphill
country. No horseman with a lick of sense or
feeling ran a horse uphill.

There were shadows. Forested country rarely
got fully daylight and after sundown the shadows
closed ranks. Sam knew the way but he was careful.

He watched for his cousin but Emory did not
appear, and that was cause for wariness. A horse
nickered. Sam swung off and led his animal. He

also tugged loose the tie-down thong over his holstered Colt.

He was approaching the camp as quietly as possible when his cousin spoke. 'Glad you could make it. Me'n Moe here been worryin' somethin' might have got in the way.'

There was no mistaking the expression on Fedderson's face when he saw Sam. He was holding a tin cup to his mouth. It stopped midway.

Emory smiled. 'I told him a friend of his was goin' to meet us. We been havin' quite a talk the last hour or so.'

Emory watched Sam hobble his horse and walk slowly back. Moses Fedderson gave the impression of a very worried man trying not to show it. As Sam sank down Emory addressed Fedderson. 'This here is my cousin, Sam Saddler. My name isn't Jones, it's Emory Saddler.'

Fedderson slowly lowered the tin cup; he put a long look on Emory who smiled as he spoke to Sam. 'He was huntin' cattle. I come along in time to help him with a pair of snorty bulls. I told him a friend of his wanted to see him. We rode up here together. Mister Fedderson's a real sensible feller, Sam.'

The leather man looked straight at Fedderson when he said, 'An' a pretty good liar.' When Fedderson would have spoken Sam held up a hand and spoke first. 'How did you get word to Mister Watson Jake Smith was with me when we visited you?'

Fedderson might not have been a very good liar but he was a very fast improviser. He stared at Sam through a moment of silence during which Sam told him what had happened to Jake Smith. What the announcement produced was an even longer silence before Fedderson said, 'They was leavin' town. Mister Smith an' his rangeboss. I was in the buggy and went after 'em.'

'An' told 'em Jake had switched sides, an' was helpin' me?'

'He did, didn't he?'

'No he didn't an' you got him killed,' Sam replied and added a little more. 'He's no loss but if you're interested he didn't have the answers I wanted. He told me that straight out and I believed him.'

Fedderson retrieved the coffee cup, held it but made no attempt to raise it. He said, 'I told your cousin about all I know.'

Sam shook his head. 'About bein' in the alley when Ambrose was killed?'

'Yes. An' some more.'

Sam slowly drew his six-gun and cocked it. 'You're a trigger pull from bein' a dead son of a bitch, Mister Fedderson. *Who shot Ambrose?*'

Emory was as still as a stone. Both Saddlers watched the rancher and waited. Fedderson answered so softly his voice barely carried. 'Al Fisher.'

'You saw him do it?'

'No, not exactly. I was goin' into the runway when he was comin' in from out back. He stopped an' said, "not a gawddamned word, you understand"?'

'That's all?' Emory asked.

Fedderson nodded. 'I went out back. Ambrose was face-down dead.'

For some seconds there was silence, then out on

the postage-stamp-sized meadow a horse squealed. The men ignored it. Fedderson remembered the cup in his hand, raised it, drained it and put it aside.

Sam had another question. 'What's your connection with Watson?'

'He give me a hundred cows on a long-term note, to be repaid out of calves. I was down to starvin' out.'

'You an' him was friends?'

'After what he done for me'n my boy I owed him, same as you would have.'

'Did you see him after the killin'?'

'He rode over the next day an' we talked.'

'Did he say why Ambrose was murdered?'

'No. Nothin' was said about that. He said he'd tore up the note; said I didn't owe him nothin'.'

Sam and Emory exchanged saturnine looks before Sam asked another question. 'Why did he have Ambrose killed?'

'Mister Saddler, I'll tell you the gospel truth: I don't know.'

'But you could guess.'

'Gossip is all, an' it amounted to whispers. Ten different reasons, mostly that Ambrose had been askin' for it a long time an' he finally got it. There's even talk you killed him.'

Emory finally spoke while looking steadily at the cowman. 'There's somethin' you might want to consider, Mister Fedderson. You meetin' Mister Watson's gunfighter in the barn means you'd be the only person who could make sense out of the killin', an' from what I know about gunfighters, they kill witnesses. You thought about that?'

Fedderson used a shirt cuff to wipe sweat off his forehead and it was not that warm a night. 'It come to me, Mister Saddler. I figured to hunt up Mister Watson before he commences his drive north an' swear to him on my ma's grave I'd never mention meetin' Fisher in the barn.'

Emory pulled a sour smile. 'You think that'll save your bacon? I don't. An' you got a boy.'

Sam gazed steadily at the ground. He seemed unaware of the exchange between Fedderson and his cousin. When he looked up he again addressed the cowman. 'How long you been in this country?' he asked.

'Nine years. My woman's buried here. My boy was mostly raised here.'

'An' your cattle have got you by?'

'Well, yes, after Mister Watson drove over the ones he give me. Done real well. I wish to Gawd my wife could've seen that, finally, we could make it.'

Sam listened to all this before bluntly saying, 'Fisher has to kill you, an' my guess is that he'll do it about the time Watson undertakes his northerly drive. You got any ideas when that'll be?'

'I'd have to guess. He ranges over hundreds of miles. In the past it's taken him maybe about a month to round 'em all up.'

'You know how long he's been gatherin' up to now?'

'Pretty close to a month.'

Sam spoke again while arising from the ground. 'Might be a good idea for you'n your lad to find a good place to hide out for a spell, Mister Fedderson.' Sam paused. 'Don't go buggy ridin' any more will you, because my cousin 'n me got reputations for eatin' fellers like Al Fisher for breakfast, an' if you hunt up Mister Watson or Fisher, we'll skin you alive and peg out the hide on the side of your house.'

Fedderson and Emory also arose. The cowman used his cuff to wipe sweat off again as he looked straight at Sam. 'We'll disappear for a spell. Until the Watson drive is out of the country anyway.'

'Maybe longer,' Sam said. 'Fisher's kind don't bother with drivin' cattle when they got a witness to get shed of. Stay hid until you hear it's safe. Make it good. Fisher's kind reads sign like a wolf. If you disappear he'll guess why an' hunt you down.' Sam nodded. Fedderson and Emory watched him go to the little meadow, unhobble the thoroughbred, rig out, mount and without a rearward glance begin picking his way back down out of the darkened uplands.

Emory said, 'He's the best there is, Mister Fedderson, an' he's something else; a man plays square with him, he never forgets.'

Fedderson was thinking of four dead *bandoleros* when he replied, 'I don't think I'd want to be wearin' Fisher's boots.'

Emory smiled, took the cowman out to the horses, waited until Fedderson was astride, then said, 'You got to make up a good story why you been gone so long. The boy'll wonder. By the way, did you teach him to draw an' shoot?'

'He learned by himself.'

'Too bad,' Emory replied, swinging across leather. 'When you're young you think you're bullet proof, but you aren't. A word of advice, Mister Fedderson, like Sam said, don't even think of huntin' up Watson or Fisher. From up here I can see even when you go out back to pee.'

Emory left the meadow riding westerly. Fedderson, who had been saddling horses all his life missed catching the cinch twice and did what to horsemen was inexcusable, he struck the horse's teeth during the bitting.

He was the last rider to leave the uplands, and rode without haste concocting the lie he had to tell his son.

Sweat bothered him all the way down to flat country in the direction of his yard, and by the time he reached the barn to care for his animal and saw the flickering lamplight from the house, he used the soggy cuff one more time.

7

The Hunt Begins

Sam had not been especially surprised to learn who had murdered his father. But why Ambrose had been killed bothered him. In time he would return to the subject of Watson and his rangeboss.

The blacksmith of Saddler's Wells was a wrinkled, prune-like individual with pale-blue eyes, a bear-trap mouth and thinning hair usually hidden beneath a visored, quilted cap.

His shop was south of Rattlesnake's barn and corrals. It had been in operation many years. Those who might have questioned this had only to stroll as far as the rear doorway beyond which was an assortment of discarded light and heavy wheels, twisted axles, mounds of horseshoes which imperiled gropers with rusty protruding nails. There were even occasional rare ox-shoes.

It was the ox-shoes that certified how long the smithy had existed as it also hinted at the age of the stringy, rawhide-like individual who owned and operated it.

If Walt Lacy had ever had a woman no one, not even other old-timers, could recall it. He was a moderate drinker, as anyone who spent time every day leaning over was entitled to be; human backs were not designed for blacksmithing.

Walt was noted for his proficiency at his trade. There was no better smith for hundreds of miles in all directions. This guaranteed his survival as a blacksmith. His disposition, or more properly, his character, put some folks off a little. Even in the freewheeling world which existed on the frontier, unless dissent was popular, dissenters were unlikely to have hordes of friends.

Walt took Sam Saddler to his grimy small office, showed Sam where to sit, on one of the up-ended horseshoe kegs, offered a cigar which Sam declined, lighted up one for himself and peered at Saddler, a mere boy to a man as old, scarred and experienced as Walt Lacy, and said, 'Well now, I wondered how long it'd take. I expect you talked to that tall feller whose horse I shod. Nice feller, friendly as a setter pup, talks good. He could charm a bird down out'n a tree.'

Walt paused to expectorate on the earthen floor and plug the stogie back into its wet place. 'Things stick in a man's craw until he can't swaller good. What did the tall feller tell you?'

Sam eyed the older man cautiously. 'Why would I have to talk to some stranger?'

'Because you're settin' there, boy, an' the tall feller's the onliest man I really got it all out of my craw to.' Lacy shifted the stogie from one side of his mouth to the other while awaiting Sam's next words.

'Ambrose was my pa.'

'That's no surprise to folks.'

'I never knew him.'

'Just as well. He was a worthless old drunk with a mean disposition.'

'If he was drunk the night he got killed—'

'Boy, Ambrose was never plumb sober.'

'Why would someone gun down an old man who couldn't even find his gun let alone use it?'

'Drunks can be dangerous, mainly ones that know things some folks would as soon no one knew about.'

'About wagonloads of contraband guns?'

Walt's stogie slid to the other side of his mouth again. 'You did talk to the tall feller,' he said.

'He's my cousin. Ambrose was his uncle.'

That time the palpable surprise did not cause the cigar to shift but it made the pale-blue eyes widen. 'He's in town?'

'No. Let's get on to what you told him.'

'Not much to tell. Ambrose done odd jobs after he no longer drove freight for Art Carlyle. Begged a little too. I figure it was havin' to beg that burnt out the last of his self-respect and turned him mean. Anyway, a mean-mouthed drunk was dangerous to them as hired him to run guns.'

'Did he take 'em to the border?'

'Nope. The wagons was parked in Mister Carlyle's big warehouse out back. At night they was taken out an' drove away through the alley behind my yard. I heard 'em. Never been a hard sleeper after comin' within inches of gettin' scalped. They went south. You know how far it is to the border from here?'

'No.'

'One night an' one day's drive.' Walt removed the cigar to expectorate again. 'You be interested in somethin' else I figured? Out of the whole cloth, mind you. There's no way to prove it because you killed all but one an' that son of a bitch took wing. I figured them *bandoleros* wasn't really after you, they was up here to hide out until it was wagon-drivin' time.' Lacy's eyes narrowed. 'You know somethin' else, boy? I haven't heard a wagon go down my alley since you shot up them border jumpers.'

Sam leaned forward, both hands between his knees in a bent forward position trying to remember where he'd heard the gun-running business was no longer in operation.

Walt misinterpreted Sam's thoughts and said, 'If you go after Ambrose's killer, boy, you better sprout an eye in the back of your head because as sure as night follers day, whoever done the killin' didn't do it on his own. There'll be trouble.'

'Any ideas?' Sam asked looking up.

The smith had to relight his cigar, which took time, and when he had a decent head of smoke rising someone walked in from out front leading a horse. Lacy left the dark little office. Sam listened as the horseman and the blacksmith discussed a reshoeing job.

Sam expected the smith to return. Instead he led the horse farther into his shop near the anvils and forge, and while pumping up red coals engaged the horse's owner in conversation.

Sam gave it up, waited until the horse's owner's back was to the roadway, then left. Walt Lacy saw him leave and remained expressionless.

Back at the leather works Sam tossed his hat
aside, leaned on the counter and saw a scribbled-on
scrap of paper which said the Watson cow outfit
was striking camp, that the drive was underway
trailing north.

He went out back looking for fresh shod horse
marks and found none. If Emory hadn't left that
scrap of paper he couldn't imagine who might have
done it, went back inside and was pocketing the
paper when he looked on its reverse side. There
were two initials: MF.

Irritation mounted. He had distinctly told Moses
Fedderson to take his boy and go to ground. It only
occurred to him when he went south for his
thoroughbred that Fedderson had demonstrated
good faith by sneaking into town and leaving the
note.

He rode north with fading daylight, reached the
uplands while there was still sunlight and followed
his own sign directly to his cousin's camp.

It was empty. Even the canteen was gone. There
was no sign of a hasty departure, bundles of food
were still hanging from low tree limbs.

He hobbled the horse in the small empty
meadow, got comfortable with shadows forming,
and waited. It was a long wait, almost too long. He
was preparing to leave when he heard a shod hoof
strike stone. Moments later his cousin appeared,
and nodded without speaking until after he'd
cared for his horse, then strolled back removing his
gloves. He still said nothing until he had motioned
for Sam to sit, sank down himself, and said,
'Watson's started his northward drive.'

Sam nodded as he wordlessly handed over the

scribbled note which his cousin read, saw the
initials on the back and handed it back with a sour
comment. 'Damned idiot. He'll get himself killed
sure as hell.' After a moment's silence the tall man
said, 'I had a hunch, rode the rims until I seen the
dust.' He gazed across the fire ring. 'Fisher'll be up
there, or maybe not. Maybe he'll come lookin' for
Fedderson.'

Sam nodded. 'Which one goes with the drive an'
which one hunts the son of a bitch back here?'

'I'll go with the drive. You'd do better to hunt
him up down here. Folks know you, they wouldn't
know a stranger.'

'I talked to the blacksmith.'

Emory solemnly replied. 'That's another one
Fisher'll want. If he talked to me, a stranger, he's
talked to others. Fisher's type don't miss no bets at
coverin' their back trail, do they?'

Sam changed the subject. 'There's still the
storekeeper, but he can wait.'

Emory replied as he was arising, 'The
storekeeper most likely didn't know about the
murder until afterwards. That's a guess. We can
talk to him after we find Fisher.'

'And Watson.'

Emory nodded. 'And Watson.'

As Sam also arose he said, 'There'll be Watson's
other riders.'

Emory smiled for the first time. 'You act like I
come down in the last rain.'

Sam also smiled. 'Maybe. But there's not many of
us left.'

Emory went with his cousin out to the small
pasture and was silent until Sam was astride, then

he said, 'If I was lookin' for that rangeboss, I'd do it at the Fedderson place.'

Sam nodded. 'Thanks, Emory. I'd never have thought of that.'

The ride back was without haste, and in fact Sam did not arrive in town until the moon was high. He had made a side trip to the locale of the Fedderson yard, waited almost an hour for a sign he might not be alone out there before giving up. Fedderson was gone, the corralled horses had been turned out and there was no light at the house.

If the gunfighter turned up he was going to find what Sam had found – nothing.

By the time he rode into Rattlesnake's runway where one smoking old unwashed lamp mantle cast puny light, he and his big horse were both tired.

There was no sign of Rattlesnake but there was no need for him. Sam cared for his animal, considered a feeble light showing from the parlour of the Harris house, and decided he would eat at the Chinee's place. There was a light there too, but no customers. In fact the proprietor was wearily cleaning up his kitchen. He had neglected to lock the roadway door. When Sam walked in the caféman sang out in irritable and barely comprehensible English that the eatery was closed.

Sam sank down at the counter, struck the wood twice with the butt of his six-gun and when the caféman came from behind his curtain, Sam said, 'Whatever you got, and black coffee.'

The proprietor ducked back from sight and in an exclamation of diminishing indignation and barely comprehensible English said, 'You break counter you pay!'

Saddler's Wells had a reputation for bedding down with the chickens, except for single men, and an occasional married one who ruled at home with an iron fist, and these individuals congregated at the only business establishment that functioned under bright lamps after sensible folks had bedded down.

Sam finished eating, paid up and told the eatery owner good night. The response was a hissing sound and a glare. He went north in the direction of the saloon.

There were about a dozen customers, some had been drinking, some seemed too tired to do more than stare at their faces in the back-bar mirror, but when Sam walked in and the big Greek boomed a hearty welcome, the customers stirred.

Sam recognized one stockman among the townsmen. The individual who had whispered to old man Watson and his rangeboss at the Mexican stand off in Watson's cow camp some time earlier. He saw the look on the rangeman's face and correctly interpreted it. Apprehension.

Spartas set up a bottle and a jolt glass and beamed. 'I sent you some business this afternoon,' he exclaimed. 'Some freighters with busted harness. Only you wasn't there. They said they'd look you up in the morning.'

Sam downed the liquor, waited for the rush of energy which usually arrived, and it did not emerge. Spartas refilled the little glass, and Sam turned it idly in its little sticky pool looking at himself in the mirror. He looked almost as weary as he felt.

The Watson rider pushed his glass away and was

turning to depart. Sam allowed him to almost reach the doors then said, 'What did you tell Mister Watson an' the rangeboss when we had that stand off over my shot-out window at Watson's camp?'

The rider, a grizzled, rock-hard looking man, faced back around. 'I reminded 'em you was the feller that shot it out with them *bandoleros* some time back. I told the old man you'n Spartas could make a right smart stand despite the odds.'

Sam gazed at the man. 'What's your name?'

'Jet Curtin.'

'How come you're not with the drive?'

'The old man sent me to pick up some coffee an' the mail. I'll catch up tomorrow.' Jet Curtin made an attempt to smile. 'Runnin' out of java on a drive makes men ornery. You know how that is?'

Sam ignored the question. 'Who come to town with you?'

Curtin's look of astonishment was genuine. 'No one. Just me.'

'When did you leave the drive?'

'As it was gettin' lined out this mornin'.'

'You want to be on your way?'

'Sure do.'

'Then answer me a question: did Mister Watson and the rangeboss do a lot of palaverin'?'

Jet Curtin seemed either unwilling or unable to give an answer he thought Sam wanted, so he took the middle of the road. 'They always palaver.'

'Yesterday more'n other times?'

Again the hard-faced rangeman hesitated. 'I was out bringin' in the drag until late.'

'Was either Watson or Fisher out too?'

'Not with me they wasn't.'

Sam said, 'Shed your gun.'

Curtin did not obey immediately, which may have been attributable to the fact that the abrupt change of conversation baffled him, or he might have had another reason, but as he and Sam looked steadily at one another, Curtin lifted out the weapon and let it fall. The noise when it struck the floor was the only audible sound. Even the usually noisy big Greek neither moved nor spoke.

Sam spoke over his shoulder to the Greek without looking away from the rangeman. 'You got a place where I can lock this gent up for a few days?'

Spartas did not reply, the prune-faced blacksmith did. He had been standing at the farthest end of the bar where the light was poor. 'I got a place.'

Sam almost smiled. 'Can you lock it so's he can't get out?'

'Yep, an' it's double walled.'

'Take him down there, Mister Lacy, an' lock him up for a few days. Whatever he eats I'll pay for … Mister Curtin, don't do nothin' foolish. It'll only be for a day or two.'

'I didn't do nothin',' the rangeman retorted. 'I never got involved in anything but with the cattle. Mister, they'll miss me.'

Sam agreed with that. 'Most likely. As you said, drivin' cattle needs black java. Maybe they'll come lookin' for you. Whether they do or not, if you walk out of here you'll bust your butt to find Mister Watson an' tell him about our meetin', and right now I'd as lief you couldn't do that.'

The blacksmith crossed to the doorway, scooped

up the rangeman's gun, cocked it and jerked his head.

For a long time after the two men had left no one spoke. But after Sam departed, not for his bed at Widow Harris's place but for the hayloft of Rattlesnake's barn, one of the more garrulous townsmen made a comment. 'I wouldn't mess with that leather man.'

Another customer at the bar took it up by saying, 'I smelt somethin' goin' on lately.' The speaker's eyes brightened. 'You don't expect it's because of Ambrose an' this Saddler bein' related?'

He got no speculation. Chris Spartas removed his short apron, tossed it atop the bar, which was an indication he was ready to call it a day and close up. His lingering customers emptied their glasses and trooped out into the night like penguins, one after the other.

Chris groped beneath the bar, located the small odd-shaped bottle, poured a jolt glass full of some dark, viscous liquor, raised it briefly in the direction of the doorway, tipped his head back and downed the molasses-like liquor, let it all roll out, put the glass in a tub of greasy water, also under the bar, got a cigar from a locked drawer and before going to his lean-to quarters out back, blew all the lamps out.

For Sam, after a side-trip to the smithy to locate the old double-walled storehouse which was now securely padlocked with a device as large as a man's palm, he leaned and spoke quietly. 'Had to do it, Mister Curtin. You'll be fine for a few days.'

The answer came showing no indignation. 'I told you, I never got mixed up in whatever the boss or

Al Fisher did on the side. I hired on as a rider an'
that's all I ever done.'

Sam replied dryly, 'Sure it is. Except you warnin'
them about me.'

'Well hell, I done you both a favour. Al Fisher's
got one hell of a reputation. Besides, when a man
hires on he just naturally is loyal, ain't he?'

'Good night, Mister Curtin.'

Rattlesnake's loft had been recently filled with
aromatic timothy hay, the kind some knowledgeable individual had put up at exactly the right time,
not only had it cured perfectly but unlike most
grass hay, it still retained a faint green colour. A
man could find no better place to bed down.

Sam was asleep almost before he shed his hat,
boots and weapon-belt.

He only awakened when he heard Rattlesnake
speaking. Rattlesnake had climbed to the loft to
fork hay into mangers below. He was leaning on
the four-tine hay fork, staring, when he said,
'Widow Harris throw you out? I just come from the
eatery. There was talk about you makin' trouble at
the saloon last night.'

Sam sat up brushing off hay. Rattlesnake offered
Sam his hat after shaking chaff out of it. He said,
'Mind the boots. I got mice up here.'

Sam stood up, dropped on the hat, shook out the
boots before stamping into them and was buckling
the gunbelt around his middle when he smiled at
the liveryman-trader. 'My pa told me a long time
ago, no one who smoked should ever bed down in a
hayloft.'

Rattlesnake's rejoinder was basic. 'I've never seen
you smoke.'

'I don't. I tried it several times and got sicker'n a dog. I admire folks that didn't give up as easy as I did.'

Sam was backing down the loft ladder when Rattlesnake asked a question. 'You want your horse?'

'I'll get him, an' thanks for the use of the loft.'

Rattlesnake abandoned the hay fork and also descended the ladder. On the runway floor he said, 'I heard at the Chinee's place you got Walt to lock up a rangeman last night.'

Sam smiled as he rigged out the thoroughbred. 'You ought to know, Rattlesnake, small towns got more imagination than a man can shake a stick at. See you later.'

'You ain't had breakfast!'

Sam waved from the saddle, walked the thoroughbred a solid mile before boosting him over into a lope. The morning had a diminishing chill, the sky was flawless, a man could see almost the far curve of the world.

8

A Meeting

It was a long shot. Maybe not a very good one, but as both Sam and his cousin knew, men who murdered could not leave folks behind who suffered from verbal dysentery.

Any approach to the Fedderson place was across open grassland. Sam squinted against morning brilliance. He was loose in the saddle but nowhere else, and the tie-down hung free of the holster.

Possibly the chances were about equal Fisher would not be out here, but no man in his right mind rode toward a possible killing without expecting to find that odds didn't matter as much as survival did.

Fedderson's range was flat to rolling. In the distance there were horse-high boulders, close-spaced as though in prehistoric times whatever had placed them had done so with just enough force and momentum to leave them grouped.

Sam speculated about Fedderson and his boy. If

the father had a lick of sense he would expect the
gunfighter to head for the rock pile after
ascertaining neither of the Feddersons was in the
yard. It was the only logical place for the
Feddersons to hole up. At least as far as Sam could
see. But he didn't know the territory and there
were arroyos and erosion washes in several
directions.

His interest was not in the Feddersons. He and
his cousin had done all they could to warn the
cowman. The closer he got to the yard the more
intently his eyes studied buildings, corrals, even the
unkempt, shaggy old shade trees.

Fisher would have stalled his horse and if he
knew the identity of the oncoming rider, and had a
rifle, or even a carbine, he'd have an advantage.

It would be foolish to rely on a gunfighter's pride
about facing his victims, because about as many –
maybe more – dead victims of gunmen had been
shot from a distance.

A brush rabbit as large as a house cat sprang
from the grass and made a zigzag rush with its ears
pinned back. The thoroughbred flinched and
missed a lead, but those were things to be expected.

When Sam was not too far south of the yard he
reined so that the house would be between him and
anyone watching from an outbuilding or the barn.

It would not advance his chances if Fisher was in
the house.

Several noisy and raffish crows swooped low.
Two landed atop the barn, their companions
lighted atop the house.

This wasn't farmed country; crows might make a
stop to rest in grass country, but their customary

hovering place was where someone had planted grain.

Sam distinctly heard them making their scolding racket. He did not take his eyes off the rear of the house. A gun shoved past a window would reflect sunlight.

What eventually happened was the result of the rest-stop of those crows. One crow left the barn's ridge, reached the ground and commenced foraging. His friend above squawked, spread wings and settled in corral dust to join the first crow scathing and foraging. The first crow had a cranky and acquisitive nature, not unusual in crows. He squawked and flew at the second crow, who, caught unprepared, also squawked as he sprang into the air to flee.

He passed through the barn's doorless rear opening still squawking. His pursuer banked away. As pursuer he had leeway for decisions. The crow that flew inside the barn was fleeing from attack.

Sam knew only that the pair of birds atop the house abruptly became noisily agitated. When Sam was closer they sprang into the air to fly easterly.

Sam was close enough to the rear of the house to make a perfect target when he swung to the ground, palmed his Colt and keeping the horse between himself and the house, was taken by surprise when something struck the inside of the barn with enough force to make dust fly.

Sam edged to the nearest corner and peeked around. A large crow was making enough noise to rouse the dead as he shot into the yard from the doorless front barn opening.

Moments later a small crow also came out of the

barn. This one did not make a sound, he was fleeing for his life, or thought he was.

Sam heard the squawking diminish as time passed. What interested him was the thunderous noise from inside the barn.

A horse could have made it, perhaps startled by the crows. If a horse was not in the barn, then Sam had no idea what could have made that sound. He had heard horses kick inside barns most of his life and, as he remained mostly hidden at the south-west corner of the house, he would have bet his life that had been a horse.

He sank to one knee listening and watching when it occurred to him that he damned well might just be betting his life for a fact.

The Feddersons could have left a stalled horse although that was unlikely. There was a thousand-to-one chance one of Fedderson's turned-loose horses had come back. Among horsemen these animals were known by two particular designations, 'barn sour' and 'home-comers'.

Sam's horse still midway along the rear wall, stamped his foot, not because he was bored, but because deer flies were bothering him, and deer flies stung like a bee.

Sam leaned back to mop sweat off and look back. The thoroughbred had evidently routed his annoyers, he was now trying to investigate some scraggly geraniums growing where wash water was flung away.

Almost sure there was a stalled or tied horse in the barn, and equally as convinced it was not a Fedderson animal, that left a good possibility that whoever owned that animal had put it where it would be out of sight, and that could very well mean the gunfighter was either in the barn or close by.

If Fisher was here, then he must not have been here long, otherwise he would have determined the Feddersons were gone and would have also left.

If he had been here for any length of time he would certainly have seen Sam approaching over miles of open country. There was one other possibility, if he had not been here long he might have been caring for his animal in the barn, in which case it was probable that he had not seen Sam, who raised up slowly considering the outbuildings between himself and the barn.

If Fisher was here he had to find him. He might have escaped detection on the way in, but that kind of luck might not hold when he left, crossing open country again. He had to satisfy himself one way or another, so he studied the outbuildings for a way to reach the barn undetected.

He was startled by the thoroughbred nickering, something horses rarely did unless they had seen, or scented, something they identified with.

Sam whirled. There was nothing but the thoroughbred in sight. He leaned against the siding to hear movement in the house. There was silence.

He returned to figuring out how to reach the barn without being seen, and because of areas of separation between what were a storehouse, a well-house and a three-sided smithy, there was no way he could be concealed the full distance.

He did not have to be told that old man Watson's rangeboss was a deadly adversary.

The sun was passing away westerly. It was late afternoon. Sam dried a sweaty palm down the side of his britches, regripped the Colt and with full lungs ran to the nearest outbuilding. His arrival stirred up a large paper nest of yellow jackets. He stood perfectly still while the agitated flying insects coursed around but did not land.

From the well-house with its wasps to the next outbuilding was about fifteen feet. He had an advantage. By sidling along the rear of the well-house then moving into the shelter of the north wall, the next shed was squarely in front of him. No one could see him from the barn.

The three-sided smithy offered similar protection once he reached it, but this time the distance was greater, more than fifty or sixty feet.

He was poised to make the dash when the muted ring of spur rowels froze him. The sound seemed to come from either outside or in the framing of the doorless front barn opening, and this time it could not be anything but another man.

He began to believe he and whoever was in the barn had arrived simultaneously. If they hadn't, if the other man had arrived earlier he surely would not have remained in the barn. Not if he was seeking the Feddersons.

His thoughts were scattered when someone cleared his pipes and expectorated, an act men did not do who worried about detection.

Whoever he was, he did not appear to be suspicious nor worried. Sam eased along the rear of the shed, reached the northerly corner, strained to hear, and slowly eased his head around.

It was Alton Fisher and he was standing in clear view about a dozen or so feet out front of the barn's doorless opening.

Sam watched as the rangeboss went to work making a smoke. When he had licked it closed and put it between his lips he hoisted a leg to strike the match, Sam could have shot him at any time during that period.

Fisher faced the house trickling smoke. Without haste he started in that direction, which gave Sam an opportunity to sidle along the north wall of the shed and watch Fisher reach the porch.

Sam heard Fisher's fist rattle the door, not once but three times, after which the rangeboss squeezed the latch and shoved the door open.

He did not enter immediately, he turned to scan the yard and beyond from the porch, considered his quirly, dropped it, stamped it out and entered the house.

As sure as night followed day if Fisher made any kind of a search he was going to either see or hear the thoroughbred horse tied out back.

Sam regretted not calling Fisher when he'd had the chance.

It was a long wait but eventually the rangeboss emerged and paused again to scan the area from the porch. Now, the tie-down was hanging loose on his holster. Now too, he neither moved nor acted as relaxed and easy as he'd acted before.

He surprised Sam when he called out. 'Come out where I can see you, you son of a bitch.'

Sam straightened up, let the tie-down thong hang loose and was preparing to move into sight when Fisher called again. 'Fedderson, you double-crossin' bastard, hidin' ain't goin' to help. The old man done you favours, more'n I'd have done, an' you done what Smith done – bit the hand that fed you. Fedderson, I'm comin' for you.'

Fisher stepped to the edge of the porch and teetered there before starting down the steps.

Sam took down a deep breath, let it out slowly and moved clear of the shed in plain sight. At first Fisher did not see him because he was looking in the opposite direction, but when his head swung and he saw Sam he stopped stone still. For several seconds they regarded each other then Fisher's right shoulder sagged slightly and that was when Sam twisted sideways and fired.

Fisher staggered, caught his balance and with his six-gun rising Sam shot again. Fisher's gun thundered, the bullet ploughed a trough five feet in front of the leather man, his knees gave way and he went down, but his six-gun swung for another shot, and this time Sam fired as he moved left, and with either luck or exceptional timing the bullet followed a blind course northward out of the yard.

Sam went toward the downed man, his cocked six-gun pointing directly at Fisher's head. The ground was bloody, Fisher seemed unable despite a formidable will, to do more than let the six-gun slide from his fingers.

Sam kicked it away, put up his own gun and looked steadily at the man looking directly back and swearing in a breathless tone of voice. Sam's first strike had grazed Fisher's right side, the shirt was red-soggy. His second shot had struck the rangeboss in the soft parts. The third slug had gone through and had broken Fisher's back.

Sam sighed. 'Whatever Mister Watson paid you, it wasn't worth this.'

'Gawddamn preacher, you got some whiskey?'

Sam shook his head and hunkered. Fisher was bleeding but less outwardly than inwardly. Sam stood up, scooped up the rangeboss's six-gun, threw it as far as he could and went to the house.

The whiskey was in a tan jug someone had plugged with a corn cob. Sam returned to the yard with it. During his absence Fisher had weakened. His hoarsely defiant voice was less forceful and words ran into each other.

The whiskey helped, his eyes brightened. Even his profanity was clearer. He waited until Sam had pulled back with the jug before saying, 'I didn't figure you right, Saddler.'

Sam took a swallow from the jug too before setting it aside. 'I'll carry you to the porch where the sun won't be in your eyes,' he said, and Fisher shook his head. 'Gawddamn do-gooder! Leave me be. You snuck up on me.'

Sam nodded.

'My damned legs don't work.'

Sam gazed at the bloody wound nearly dead centre and said, 'Your back's broke.'

Fisher accepted that. 'A man with a broke back won't never walk again. You should've aimed a little higher.'

'I didn't aim,' Sam said, and changed the subject. 'How much did Mister Watson pay you to kill Ambrose in the alley?'

Fisher gave a delayed reply. During the brief, silent interval he listened to an inner voice that told him forty-three years of living was going to end in the dirt of a scrub ranch. He said, 'Sixty dollars.'

'He was drunk'n helpless.'

Fisher did not disagree. 'It was like shootin' fish

in a rain barrel.'

'Why did Mister Watson want him dead?'

'It warn't Mister Watson as much as it was that fidgety, snifflin' bastard who owns the mercantile.'

'Gun running?' Sam asked, and the dying man barely nodded his head. 'They had a good business goin'. Ambrose, the damned idiot, had a bad habit of shootin' off his mouth. It wasn't Frank Watson so much as it was the storekeeper. We'd only be down here until the grass dried up, then we'd go back up north. Mister Carlyle worried, kept after Mister Watson so I shot Saddler.'

Sam positioned himself so that the sun did not strike Fisher directly in the face. As he did this Fisher weakly coughed and gestured. Sam held the jug and this time the rangeboss swallowed five or six times. When Sam put the jug aside Fisher's face reddened, sweat appeared and his eyes brightened as he said, 'I should've listened....'

'What?'

'I should've listened to the priest at the orphanage where my folks left me. He told me if I'd join the order'n take the oath, the Lord'd make me over. Make me forget hatin' people.'

Sam's thoroughbred whinnied from behind the house. It was tired of standing and it was also thirsty. Fisher seemed not to have heard. He looked straight at Sam. 'I never believed that story about you takin' on five Mex renegades. You know how to roll a smoke?'

Sam got the makings from Fisher's shirt pocket and rolled the cigarette. Fisher eyed it as he said, 'Camel. It's got a hump in the middle.'

Sam nodded making a weak smile. Odd thing

about dying men; they make irrelevant conversation. Sam asked about family, friends, heirs, and the gunfighter squinted past trickling smoke.

'I got none of 'em. But there's somethin' you could do for me.... Find Mister Watson an' tell him Fedderson wasn't around, so he better watch his back trail.'

Sam raised his head at a distant sound and when it was not repeated he returned his attention to the gunfighter; the bleeding seemed to be lessening, Fisher's weathered face was losing colour, his eyes seemed to be fixed on something above Sam's left shoulder. When Sam was easing back Fisher said, 'Keep the gun. It cost me six dollars to have a gunsmith work it over so's there'd be a hair trigger.'

Sam considered the jug. When he reached for it Fisher made a choking sound in his throat. When Sam looked back the rangeboss's eyes were wide open and drying. He was dead.

Sam dragged him by the feet into the barn, covered him with a soiled and patched old wagon canvas, went around behind the house, led his animal to be watered, then off-saddled both horses, turned them into the corral to roll over and back, and leaned on the stringers for a long time.

He did not search for the gun he had hurled away.

A dog coyote appeared in the yard, leery and watchful. He sniffed where the blood was, studied the buildings and with no reason Sam could imagine, whirled and raced northward in a belly-down run. The day was ending. There would still be two or three hours of daylight. When he was satisfied the horses were ready he saddled the thoroughbred, led the FW gelding and left the yard without looking back.

He rode all the way to town seeing Fisher's face and recalling his words. It was not a matter of conscience, the son of a bitch deserved to die. But it would have been better if he'd died instantly.

When he reached town dusk was close. Rattlesnake watched the unsaddling, saw the Watson mark on the left shoulder of the led horse and did not say a word. Not until Sam had cared for the animals and had left, then Rattlesnake made a beeline for Walt Lacy's smithy, where he told his story and after the blacksmith had heard it all, he dryly said, 'Are you sure it's Al Fisher's horse?'

'I've seen Fisher on that horse a hunnert times. I'm sure.'

'Well then,' stated the blacksmith, 'good riddance.'

Rattlesnake was not to be appeased that easily. 'But what about Mister Watson? He won't like his rangeboss turnin' up missing.'

Walt folded his mule-hide shoeing apron, placed it carefully across an anvil and said, 'Have you et?'

'No.'

'Well, suppose we go up to the saloon first, then go down to the eatery.'

'I ain't finished grainin' yet.'

Walt shrugged. 'Go do it. I'll be up at the saloon.'

'Don't you say anythin'. This here is my story an' it'll be worth a free round.'

Walt nodded, watched Rattlesnake scurry back to his barn, and wagged his head. He told a sooty wall that evidently the requiem for a gunfighter came down in simple terms to who told the story first, for a free drink.

The Chinee looked disapprovingly at Sam Saddler. There was nothing wrong with the steak, spuds and sliver of pie he had put before the leather man, who hadn't eaten half of it. He said, 'I make, you eat.'

Sam arose smiling. He scattered coins atop the counter and went out into the increasing darkness. It would have felt good to bed down upstairs at the Widow Harris's place on a real bed.

Instead he returned to the loft of Rattlesnake's barn.

9

Emory!

Sam worried a little about his cousin. Emory was capable enough but he had a quirk about doing things. Sometimes he grinned his way right into the barrel of a gun.

The following mid-afternoon Moses Fedderson came to town in his top buggy. He went first to the harness works where Sam was busy plaiting a pair of seven foot reins out of moistened but untanned leather, a chore not to be interrupted except for emergencies. Fedderson strode to the stove to draw off a cup of coffee before Sam was aware of his presence. They exchanged a look before Fedderson said, 'There was eighty dollars in his pockets.' Sam placed the loose ends of rawhide far enough apart so that when he returned to plaiting he would know where he had stopped, shrugged and said, 'Did you bury him?'

'Eighty dollars worth.' Fedderson considered his cup of coffee without raising it. 'Mister Watson'll fret when he don't come back.'

Sam's reply was short. 'That's the idea.'

'I come by your cousin's camp. It was empty'n his horse was gone.'

Sam stalled by going to the stove for a cup of coffee. When he was back behind the counter he said, 'He had some ridin' to do,' and changed the subject. 'It ought to be safe for you'n the lad now. All the same I'd keep watch.'

Fedderson emptied the cup, nodded and left the shop. Sam saw him enter the emporium. Eighty dollars ought to pay for enough supplies to last until next fall.

Sam kept busy at the shop until just shy of supper time, then got his thoroughbred and rode north with a couple of hours of daylight left.

When he reached the uplands he stopped once to look back. Except for a freight wagon there was no activity, no rider, and the freighter was going south toward town.

He headed for his cousin's camp without haste. There was an excellent chance Emory would not be there; it depended on how far north he had to ride to find the Watson drive.

But he was there. At least his horse was. It nickered from the little clearing. Sam did not see it until he was close to the camp clearing, and he stopped stone still. It was Emory's animal, but it was grazing with the bridle in its mouth and Emory's saddle on its back.

He tethered the thoroughbred, walked in the direction of the fire ring and was greeted with a droll comment. 'There must be easier ways to serve the Lord.'

Emory was leaning against a tree, there was blood on his shirt and britches. As Sam came forward he said, 'There's a pony of rye whiskey in my saddle-bags....'

Sam ignored that to lower himself to one knee, leaned and lifted soggy cloth. As he did this his cousin said, 'That old man's as devious as a coyote.'

Sam finished his examination, wiped his hands and looked at his cousin. 'I told you when we was kids you got confidence where you should have commonsense. Bushwhack you, did they?'

Emory said, 'In the saddle-bags, dammit!'

Sam went to the little meadow, stripped the horse, which promptly went down on all fours and vigorously rolled. Sam had to wait to put on the hobbles and rummage for the bottle. When he returned his cousin gestured for the canteen, and drank deeply from it before holding out a hand for the whiskey. Sam sat waiting. Since they'd been kids Emory could be the most exasperating individual on earth.

When he put the bottle aside he sighed and said, 'That old son of a bitch was back trackin'.' Sam nodded; he could guess why. For eighty dollars Watson would want to find his rangeboss and be told Fedderson was dead.

'I was up a side hill,' Emory said, 'weavin' in an' out of the trees. When I looked up there was three of 'em. They commenced shootin' before I made out all three of 'em. Not much chance but I shot back an' turned back to get cover. One of 'em got me in the upper leg. I out-dodged 'em an' come back here.'

Sam handed his cousin the bottle and took it

back after Emory had swallowed twice. As he put
the bottle aside he said, 'Hold still,' and leaned to
make a thorough examination of the wound. It
wasn't pretty, the bullet had sliced meat and was
still bleeding. Sam tied their bandannas together,
pulled them as tightly as he could and the bleeding
stopped. The wound was swelling.

He dried his hands again and considered his
cousin, in whom the fire water had induced a
ruddy colour and watering eyes. Emory would not
be able to sit his saddle all the way back to town.
The alternative was for Sam to find Doctor Morton
and bring him up here. As he was considering this
his cousin said, 'I don't know how far they followed
me. But that old man was braying like a mule for
them to run me down.'

'How far was you?' Sam asked.

'Three, four hours. They'd most likely give up.
They got cattle to watch.'

Sam frowned. 'Why would they jump you like
that? As far as I know Mister Watson don't know
who you are.'

'Maybe not who I am, Sam, but he sure as hell
knows by now you aren't the only one makin'
trouble about Uncle Ambrose.'

Sam had questions but at the moment they were
less important than getting Emory cared for. He
stood up as he told Emory he'd go find the
medicine man and bring him back.

Emory stirred. 'I can ride down there with you if
you'll lend me a hand.'

'You can't stand up, let alone fork a saddle.'

'Hold out your hand.'

'I'll find the doc an—'

'*Hold out your damned hand!*'

Sam held it out, hoisted his cousin to his feet and steadied him.

'Rig the horses an' lead mine back here.'

This time Sam balked. 'You know how far we got to go? You'll never make it.'

'Then I'll go as far as I can. Get the horses!'

Sam got the horses, but helping Emory astride was labour, and once he was up there, jaws locked, Sam wagged his head, mounted the breedy big horse and led Emory's animal by the reins.

It was dark by the time they reached flat country. Sam did not angle toward the road, he went beeline straight. Twice his cousin could not stifle the groans, so twice they stopped. Emory's face was sweat-shiny, there was blood on his saddle, he irritably told Sam not to stop, and by the time they had lights in sight Emory had emptied the bottle of rye whiskey.

But he made it. Just barely though. When they entered the livery barn Rattlesnake was raking. He stopped, stared and seemed to have taken root. Sam growled for help. Between them they got Emory off the horse and to the bench outside the harness room. Rattlesnake, consumed with curiosity, brought a lantern and held it low so that he and Sam could examine the injury. Rattlesnake put the lantern aside as he said, 'I'll fetch Doc,' and fled toward the roadway.

In a surprisingly strong voice Emory said, 'Is he from Missouri? They talk different.'

Sam sat on the bench shaking his head. 'You got lucky but I'm about ready to give up on you. Luck don't come often.'

In the same strong voice Sam's cousin said, 'I don't like doin' this to you, Sam, but with me out of it for a spell, an' that ol' man continuin' northward.... We could let him go an' wait for him to come back.'

'*If* he comes back, Emory. After what's happened he might not come back.'

'Well then....'

'I know. But not until you're taken care of.'

This discussion might have continued if Rattle-snake hadn't returned with Doc Morton. The older man did not look pleased about being rousted from the saloon, and when he growled for someone to hold the lantern high and bent forward, he grumpily said, 'Well now, you could tell me you was attacked by a bear, mister, or you could say you fell on a sharp rock, but if that isn't a bullet-graze I'll eat my hat. Hold still. *Dammit hold still!* It'll hurt; in my business that's what we're best at.... Hmmmm, we got to get this feller in a house an' into a decent bed. I'll go get my satchel. We'll put him to sleep before I go to work on him.' Doc straightened back. 'Take him to the widow's place. She's got room. If she gets cranky about puttin' up a shot man, tell her I want it done an' right away.'

As Doc went scuttling toward the roadway Rattlesnake said, 'You'n me can carry him, Sam. Or maybe it'd be better if I got my wheelbarrow.'

That is how they got Emory Saddler to Widow Harris's front porch. When she came out holding a lamp, and saw a man in a wheelbarrow Sam thought she would drop the lantern so he took it from her, explained what Doc had said and while she stood stiffly erect and soundless, Sam and

Rattlesnake carried Emory upstairs to an empty room and with the Widow Harris in the doorway, proceeded to divest Emory of his filthy, bloody clothing and put him to bed.

While the wheelbarrow ride must have been both uncomfortable and painful, Emory took to the bed and blankets like a duck to water. He even introduced himself, then settled in and was asleep fifteen minutes before Enos Morton returned. Doc eased the Widow Harris out of the bedroom, stripped off his coat, draped his hat from an unlighted lamp at the wall, rolled up his sleeves and opened the satchel. As he did these things he sent Rattlesnake back to his barn, told Sam to stay close with the lamp held high, and went to work.

The laudanum which put Emory to sleep must have been powerful; Sam's cousin was an inert mass of torn flesh which Doc treated as he might have treated a dead man.

It was hot upstairs, which it usually was in summertime. Opening windows did not help much. Sam mopped his face, monitored Doc, watched his cousin's facial expression, and moved the lamp every time Doc growled.

The way Sam knew time had passed was when the air outside the window felt cool. There was not a sound except for an occasional grunt from Doc Morton.

When he eventually finished and went to wash in the basin at bedside, Doc looked and acted tired. Without facing Sam he said, 'You can suture a wound like that but it's still swellin' an' if it keeps on there's a good chance it'll bust where it's sewed. I used a few stitches but mostly, because the bandage is tight, I'm hopin' the torn sides will come together enough to heal.'

Doc turned drying his hands. 'You got to make him favour that leg. No movin', no stretchin' nor strainin', otherwise it'll bust loose an' he'll be in worse shape than now. You understand, Sam? Keep that leg propped up. No standin', no movin' at all.'

'For how long?'

Doc considered Emory Saddler's relaxed face. 'He's young enough, looks healthy enough – how'n hell do I know how long? It's up to him. Well, maybe five, six weeks.'

Sam sighed inwardly. Keeping his cousin immobile for five or six weeks would be just about impossible. But Sam nodded. He'd do the best he could.

Doc shrugged into his coat, snapped the satchel closed and stood a moment regarding Sam. 'How'd he get shot?'

'Run on to some men who started shootin' as he ran.'

Doc was briefly occupied peeling tinfoil off a cigar, and after biting off one end and plugging the stogie into his mouth he regarded Sam dourly and sceptically, opened the door and let himself out.

The Widow Harris, hair combed but still wearing her bath robe, was waiting in the parlour. She caught Doc before he reached the roadside door. 'Well, Enos?'

Doc wanted to get outside so he could light the cigar. 'Well, what, ma'am?'

'Is he an outlaw, because I will not have—'

'I don't know what he is,' Doc replied, gripping the doorknob. 'Ask Sam the harness maker.'

'How long before he can be moved, Enos?'

Doc was usually perverse, it was his nature, but this time he felt better the moment he answered. 'Five, six weeks. Maybe more. Depends on how fast he mends. I'd say a feller his age an'—'

'Five or six weeks! Enos, I want that man out of my house tomorrow, the day after tomorrow at the latest. What will folks think, me keepin' a shot man, maybe an outlaw?'

Doc turned the knob. 'Eunice, if he moves an' opens that wound he could bleed to death! Good night!'

Doc did not even wait to reach the roadway to light up. He did it with his back to the door on the porch.

Sam was sitting at bedside dozing when the Widow Harris rapped on the door. He glanced first at his cousin, who remained dead to the world, before opening the door.

The Widow Harris drew herself up, crossed her arms and spoke from the doorway. 'Mister Saddler, do you have living-quarters at the harness shop?'

Sam nodded.

'I can't keep him here. Doctor Morton said he might be laid up for better'n a month. I can't have a man staying here that long. I take in travellers mostly. I'm not prepared to keep a man more than a night or two.'

Sam regarded the handsome, indignant woman. 'He can't be moved. Doc said if the wound busts open he could bleed to death.'

She nodded curtly about that. Doc had told her

the same thing. 'He could be moved on a stretcher, Mister Saddler. There's one at the general store. Four men to carry it could take him up to your place.'

Sam shook his head. 'I'll pay for his room an' board. He's my cousin.'

The Widow Harris seemed briefly startled about the relationship but when next she spoke she mentioned the other matter. 'For him to stay here for a month or more, an' for me to feed him three times a day, would cost a small fortune.'

Sam thought he saw a weakening in the widow-woman's obduracy: money. He answered her quietly, 'Whatever it costs, Missus Harris.'

She hesitated. 'But not for any five or six weeks, an' if you don't mind I'd like some money in advance.'

Sam almost smiled. 'If you'll watch him I'll go to the shop an' fetch back some money.'

The woman nodded briskly and remained in the bedroom doorway until Sam was gone, then warily eyed Emory, went to the bedside chair, took it back a short distance and primly sat.

It was dawn-chilly. She considered the open window and was arising to close it when the relaxed face on the pillow spoke. 'I'll do my damnedest not to be no trouble, ma'am.'

She stood at the foot of the bed looking down. 'You were awake?'

'Yes'm. Nothin' else to do but listen to you'n Sam.'

'You could have said something.'

'There warn't nothin' I could say. You'n Sam was doin' right well.' When she would have gone to close the window, Emory also said, 'I didn't do any of this on purpose an' as quick as I can I'll find another place, maybe the hayloft at the livery barn, except that to get up there I got to climb a ladder.'

She closed and locked the window, faced around and looked steadily in the direction of the bed. 'I don't take in permanent boarders, only over-nighters an' the like.'

Emory gravely nodded about that. 'If there'd been another place.... As soon as I can hobble I'll leave. Right now, I got a headache; you wouldn't have a draw of liquor ...?'

'Not in this house!'

'Yes'm. Well, thank you an' as quick as I can I'll find another place.'

He waited until she departed then tested the wounded leg. The result was fierce, shooting pain. He adjusted himself to favour the leg and slept.

Sam returned after high noon to tell his cousin he would be out of town for a few days and that he'd asked Doc Morton to look in on his cousin when he could.

Emory listened to all this then said, 'They'll be watchin', Sam, an' they're a *coyote* bunch.'

Sam stood at the bedside looking down when he replied. 'A man that's forewarned is forearmed. You remember old Titus Manville sayin' that?'

'Sure do.'

'I'll be back directly,' Sam said, and got as far as the door before saying the rest of it. 'Widow Harris is a good cook. Come right down to it she's a good woman. Give her time, Emory.'

The bedridden man nodded and after Sam had departed he said aloud, 'That's what I got lots of, partner. Time.'

Doctor Morton arrived in late afternoon to see his patient. Widow Harris had three travelling salesmen in her parlour waiting for supper. They looked up when the widow woman met Doc at the door and said, 'Sam Saddler gave me one hundred dollars.'

Doc closed the door, saw the overnight travellers listening, took the widow woman by the arm as far as the kitchen before releasing her as he said, 'Nobody's paid me that much in better'n twenty years, an' then it was Confederate money not worth the paper it was wrote on.' Doc studied the woman's expression before also sayin', 'Don't look a gift horse in the mouth.'

'Enos, are you certain they aren't outlaws? Where would a harness maker get a hundred dollars?'

Doc was here for just one purpose and his intention had been to perform that purpose and get back to the Greek's place as quickly as possible. He sounded irritable when he told her where the hundred dollars came from was not important, that she had it was important, then left her standing in the kitchen to climb the stairs to his patient's room.

Emory greeted the old man by jutting his chin ceilingward. 'You got any idea how many of them little curlicues there is on the ceiling?'

Doc neither replied nor looked up. He gripped Emory's wrist, consulted his huge golden pocket watch, let go of the wrist, peeled back an eyelid, listened to the heart, stepped back to pocket his watch and ask questions. When he was satisfied with the answers he peeled back the covers to examine his handiwork.

As he pulled the covers back into place he said, 'Sam left town couple hours back ridin' north.'

If that statement was intended to elicit a revelatory response, it failed. Emory looked straight up at Doc and said, 'Did he?'

Widow Harris did not mention the one hundred dollars when she took a supper tray upstairs and as she was to learn, getting direct answers from Emory Saddler was an exercise in futility. Not only was he pleasant, friendly and co-operative but he also somehow managed to achieve control of conversations, and did it so subtly the other person hardly knew an initiative had been lost.

He told her Sam had said she was a good cook and that his cousin had been right. He also told her, that first night at the rooming-house, an old man named Ambrose Saddler had been his uncle and wondered if she had known Ambrose.

She had but seemed disinclined to be drawn into a conversation about Ambrose. Emory understood; Uncle Ambrose dead or alive did not arouse admiration.

10

A Man With Tan Eyes

For Sam night riding was no novelty, but back-tracking the men who had shot his cousin required daylight, so he took his time, stopped often and when first light arrived he was several miles northward, far enough in fact to hear lowing cattle, the kind of noise animals made when roused from their beds.

He kept below the skyline and used game trails and rode warily. For an hour or so he could not make out riders, just cattle, but eventually the man driving the camp wagon halted to make a harness adjustment, and the moment he halted a rider came loping back. Even at a distance Sam recognized the rider. He had been among the FW men in the camp when Sam and Spartas had met old man Watson.

Sam moved into deep forest shade, dismounted and watched. What had caused the halt seemed to be one of the traces. Such occurrences were not unusual and, as was customary, there was an extra tug in the wagon. It required something like fifteen minutes to make the change then, as the driver went back to his seat, the rider swung up and followed. After a brief exchange the driver fumbled until he found the bottle, passed it over and retrieved it as the rider turned to lope ahead.

Sam picked his way carefully. He tried to count the drovers, which was not always possible; large herds of cattle in desert country raised thick dust banners.

Twice he saw one rider call in the others to palaver. The last time this was done one rider left the drive heading into the same forested uplands where Sam was riding. The advantage this time was that Sam saw the rider and figured his course. Unlike Emory's meeting, this time there would be no surprise. Not to a Saddler anyway.

Sam guessed the rangeman would get as high as he could so that he could have a good view of the lower slope. Any movement would interest him.

Sam chose a game trail that angled upwards and kept on it until he could see skylining firs and pines. His estimate was that the rangeman was north about a mile. If this were so, Sam would be on the top-out before the rangeman was.

The ridge had twisted trees and places where winter winds had scoured the ground to hardpan, even in a few places all the way to bedrock.

He rode carefully. A rider might fail to hear shod hooves but his mount wouldn't.

Sam had the sun high enough and at his back, but that was a benefit only in places where sunlight could penetrate past the tops of forest giants.

Sam eventually left the thoroughbred tied in shade and scouted ahead with his Winchester. What inadvertently favoured him was a busy little waterfall which made enough noise to preclude anyone determining sound.

Sam coursed northward until he found a large pool. In this place the only sound was scolding bluejays high overhead. He went around to the east side of the pool. The trail he had used to reach this place skirted the westerly side of the pool, the normal route of someone riding northward from the westerly side hills.

His mistake was to consider the possibility that the manhunting FW rider would be riding southward along the rim using a different trail.

Sam chose an excellent place for his wait. He became as mottled as everything else around him. Sunlight penetrated in irregular patterns.

He did not see the manhunter as much as he sensed him, and he was not across the pool he was behind Sam where a very old, wide trail angled around trees on the rim.

The jay birds that had scolded Sam's arrival in their territory now raised their racket in a new direction, northward along the old elk trail.

Sam could not reach the opposite side of the pond, nor go back the way he had come even a short distance. Where he was waiting it would take good eyesight to make him out among the other mottled shapes and shadows but except for several huge old fir trees he had no real protection.

He faced the new direction and followed the FW rider's course by the denunciations being hurled at him from high above.

Once, the rider's horse struck granite with a shod forefoot. Sam estimated where the man would be when he came abreast of Sam's position, eased against one of the fir trees, raised his carbine to a hand rest, and waited.

The birds, as was their custom, leapt from tree top to tree top closely following intruders. Sam singled out a scant opening where sunlight reached and waited.

The rider stopped a hundred yards or so north of Sam's target area. Sam leaned to look rearward and northward, but moments later the rider was moving again, and Sam caught his first glimpse. The man had his saddle gun balanced across his lap. He was nondescript except for a wide horsehair hatband. His FW horse was ordinary. It was no longer sucking air from its climb to the rim. It seemed almost to be dozing along, head low, reins swaying.

It came to life at the same time the rider did when Sam said, 'Right where you are. One more step an' I'll blow your head off.'

The horse stopped of its own accord looking into the mottled area where that voice had come from. Its rider did the same, sat still seeking the owner of the voice.

'Get down! On the right side! Fling that carbine away!'

Young broke horses, always mounted and dismounted on the left side, might spook at a rider swinging off on the right side but this horse didn't, although when its rider touched down the horse eased slightly away.

Sam gave another order. 'Now the belt gun. Real

careful,' and the rider finally spoke in a voice heavy
with sarcasm. 'Real careful when I got no idea
where you are?'

Sam replied curtly, 'Tie the horse. Fine. Now
turn your back.'

The rangeman obeyed each time but when his
back was to Sam he said, 'Mister, if you got some
idea I'm a lawman – I ain't, never have been an'
never will be.'

'Why would you be a lawman?' Sam asked and
got a sharp answer. 'Who else'd be hidin' up in
here?'

Sam grounded his carbine and picked his way
until he was directly behind his captive, then raised
his six-gun and cocked it. The other man
straightened his shoulders. He said, 'Mister, you're
as safe with me as you'd be with your mother.'

Sam told the rider to face around. As he obeyed
he and Sam took measure of each other. Sam
recognized the man but had no idea what his name
was. 'How much was old man Watson goin' to pay
you if you bushwhacked me?'

The older man had a cud which he shifted from
one cheek to the other as he studied Sam. His
tan-tawny eyes did not leave Sam's face when he
replied. 'I know who you are – the harness maker
from Saddler's Wells.'

'How much, try a straight answer for once?'

The other man had an unshaven face, a wide
mouth and a nose that had been broken. 'Mister
Watson said you was the brother of that damned
fool that rode into us some days back.'

'Cousin, not brother. For the last time – how
much!'

The rangeman paused to eject his cud then said, 'He wasn't sure it'd be you or someone else who would back-track your cousin, but the old man don't trust folks nor—'

'I told you! For the last time, how much!' Sam tilted the gun barrel.

The rider considered the gun, Sam's face and said, 'Nothin', because he warn't sure there'd be anyone ... that ain't exactly right. He told me the damned fool had a brother an' he might try somethin'.' As the tawny-eyed older man's gaze held steady, he relaxed his stance and said, 'You wouldn't have a plug would you?' And when Sam shook his head the older man dryly said, "Course not, you wouldn't have.' Then he made a small smile. 'Well, pull the trigger. I got a bad back an' the standin' bothers it.'

Sam lowered the gun barrel. 'What's your name?'

'William Prescott.'

'Set down if you like.'

'No thanks. I wouldn't want it known I was shot settin' down.'

'Where is the old man goin' to set up camp?'

'Same place he always does, goin' or comin'. Up ahead some miles at a meadow with a creek runnin' through it.' The tawny-eyed man loosened still more.

'Who killed Jake Smith?'

'Al Fisher. I brought him to town. The old man told me to prop him up across the alley from your shop.' Prescott looked away from Sam for the first time and looked back. 'Mister, it's been nice visitin' with you but I got to get back.'

Sam had met many men in his lifetime but never

one quite like William Prescott. If Prescott knew what fear was he gave Sam Saddler no indication of it.

As they faced each other Sam said, 'Pick up your six-gun.'

Prescott shook his head. 'I don't think so. I heard how you shot four Messicans face to face. Mister Saddler, I'm a stockman. That's all I know. Gunfightin' – well – I've seen gunfights an' would you like to know what I think? No matter who's right or wrong, only one man walks away, an' sometimes not even one. I'm not goin' to draw against you, but if you'd like I'll hand-fight you, an' if you win I'll get on that FW horse and ride south, an' keep ridin' south until the horse'n me is grey headed.'

William Prescott hadn't acquired his broken nose in a daisy chain. He wasn't particularly impressive in build but from what Sam had seen of the man so far, Prescott had nerves of steel. He was the kind of individual who obeyed orders, worked hard for whatever outfit he rode for, and would face life, and its adversities, head on.

They were as nearly opposite as two men could be. Sam almost liked William Prescott; during his silence the older man made another proposition.

'Mister Watson'n me don't hitch horses very well. As far as I know there wasn't no cause for Jake to get killed. I figured to quit for good when we get back up north. I've rode for that old bastard close to three years. He's mean an' connivin' an' he does connivin', sly business on the side. But I'm not goin' to sell him out to you.

'But I don't like big odds against folks either.'

Prescott's gaze was hard and steady. 'You'll be goin' up against an underhanded old connivin' son of a bitch an' he won't be alone. I expect I owe you this much for not blowin' me out of the saddle. I'll go back, lie to the old man about not findin' anyone comin' after him, an' when it's about midnight I'll stampede the cattle. After that I'll go south an' keep on ridin'. What you do ain't none of my business, but if you can catch 'em one at a time.... All right, Mister Leather Man?'

Sam grinned in spite of himself and shoved out a hand. 'Mister Prescott, I hope we meet again some day.'

'Ain't likely,' the older man said as he retrieved his weapons, snugged up the cinch and swung aside. He neither nodded nor looked back.

There was the possibility that Prescott would go back and help the old man establish an ambush. If that were the case, then Sam had made one of the biggest mistakes of his life; the possibility of it being his last mistake.

He leaned on a tree and thought. William Prescott had left him feeling that Prescott would not be a party to a bushwhack, and whatever Sam decided and did, the man with the tawny eyes would be a large part of it.

He was a unique individual, no question about that. The real question was simply whether Sam should put trust in a man he had caught trying to find him, and perhaps meant to kill him. Why should he put trust in a hard-faced, steady-eyed individual he had known about half an hour?

He went back for the thoroughbred, got astride and used the same rim-trail Prescott had used. He had put himself in a position where actually, he had no alternative.

Jay birds followed him from the topmost limbs of trees. He ignored them, concentrated on following Prescott's trail until, eventually, it split off down-slope where there was no trail but the gradient was easiest on a horse.

By the time he heard cattle and eventually saw the battered old wagon in a pear-shaped meadow with smoke rising, the day was dying.

He would have given five years of his life to have had a spy glass, the figures he saw near the wagon were little more than ant-size. He tried to determine which was William Prescott and couldn't.

Before shadows deepened he scouted in three directions. His back-trail would be safe. The other directions appeared not to have had shod horses. He did ride into a clearing where an ancient burial platform stood, rags stirring with each breeze.

It was tomahawk custom to make those burial platforms, but that had been years back. He had seen them before, several times. He had also seen where posts had rotted, the platforms had collapsed and varmints had strung shrivelled remains over considerable territory.

By the time he got back to the overlooking forested uplands shadows were pulling together to form dusk. He hobbled the thoroughbred and sat on a bed of fir and pine needles overlooking the pinprick of light that was FW's supper fire.

There would be a moon, but not for awhile yet. Not until the last vestiges of a warm day yielded to night-chill.

The horse hopped among trees seeking places where resin hadn't soured the ground. What grass he found was adequate but just barely.

After full nightfall Sam cinched up and rode as silently as he could down off the rim. It was a long ride and darkness did not help in traversing country he had never seen before.

The little fire flared up, then gradually began to lose force. Where Sam finally stopped on a brushy ledge, he could make out the rope corral, the wagon, and what could have been dark places where men had bedded down.

He considered the sky, and the silver moon when it appeared. He'd had a watch once but when a green colt had stepped on a rattler and had exploded, Sam was hurled against a tree smashing his watch.

Emory carried a watch. He smiled a little. Emory also carried a clasp knife for trimming his fingernails. Emory was as fastidious as a man could be who lived out of saddle-bags.

A wolf sang northward up near the easterly rim. Both the wolf and Sam awaited the answer. There was none, nor did the old dog-wolf call again. He didn't have a watch either, but in his case it wasn't bad timing by days, it was bad timing for seasons. Female wolves had found mates months earlier.

A cow called for her calf, continued to call until the youngster found her, butted her to her feet and nudged for all it was worth on all four teats.

Cold came, the moon inexorably altered position, Sam got his horse, checked his weapons, mounted and slow-paced until he reached flat ground. By choice he'd have preferred daylight,

but the tawny-eyed rangeman had already made
that decision for Sam.

He thought about Prescott. If Watson caught
him stampeding cattle he'd kill him on sight. Sam
doubted that the old man or his riders would be
able to do that. Prescott had impressed Sam as
about as savvy an individual as they made.

A barking dog startled him into a full halt. It
shouldn't have surprised him except that he'd seen
no dog at the cow camp, and for a fact dogs were
customarily part of every cattle drive.

A bright star flamed across the underbelly of
heaven leaving a sputtering tail-race in its wake.
For as long as it flared visibility improved.

Sam was less than half a mile from the wagon
where red coals barely showed.

He heard someone cursing until the dog stopped
making a racket. He also heard restless horses in
the rope corral and that kind of agitation would
surely arouse men. Rope corrals were fine if
confined horses did not become excited, otherwise
if some wild-eyed animal hit one, rope broke. If
that happened it could usually be blamed on a
mare. They were by nature more likely to be
panicky than horses – the terms stockmen used to
define geldings.

Sam dismounted to listen. His thoroughbred,
with the scent of other horses in the roiled air,
stood erect, little ears pointing. Sam placed a hand
over the soft muzzle to stop a whinny, but the
thoroughbred was more interested in scent and
sounds than announcing his arrival in the area.

Over time the noise abated. If men had gone out
to quiet the horses they would have returned to

their soogans. Sam led his horse, with background-
ing forest on his right and numberless mounds of
bedded cattle on his left.

Patience was something he had learned early as a
young pot hunter, nevertheless every nerve in his
body was tight-strung.

But when the night exploded with gunfire he
was unprepared. Terrified cattle sprang from the
beds and ran, tails over their backs like scorpions,
men roared curses and those corralled animals ran
in circles.

The gunfire paused briefly, then resumed. Sam
nodded about that. Prescott had to reload.

The thoroughbred fidgeted until Sam growled,
then it stood still until he was in the saddle, but an
excited breedy horse requires a savvy hand on the
reins, and Sam's animal was no exception.

He headed for the wagon area in a lope, six-gun
in hand. There was pandemonium, dust and noise.
Men hurrying the bridling and saddling process
were bleakly silent. The animals they had in hand
were too agitated to be handily controlled, but
Watson and his crew were seasoned.

Sam heard a man yell, 'Where's Will?'

He got no reply, just more profanity as the old
man led off in the direction of the bedding ground
where only a few cattle remained.

Somewhere westerly, gunfire was audible over
the racket of stampeding cattle. Sam heard the FW
men up ahead, did not increase his gait although
the riders were using spurs to goad animals into a
run.

His eyes were accustomed to the night. He
wanted to find the men who had shot his cousin

one at a time. He particularly wanted to find old man Watson.

There were no more gunshots. Sam made a humourless grin. Prescott would be heading south with what remained of the night to get clear.

He had a moment or two to acknowledge his debt to the man he had met briefly and would in all probability never meet again. He wondered how Prescott would justify stealing an FW horse, something he thought would not bother the tawny-eyed man at all.

A horseman who had veered northward came up so fast Sam did not see the man until they were close. The rider called out, 'Gawddamn rustlers!'

Sam eased the thoroughbred out a few notches as he swung nearer. When they were riding stirrup the breathless FW rider turned to speak and recognized Sam. His mouth remained open, then he hitched slightly and went for his gun.

When Sam fired the FW horse shied wildly flinging its rider in a pinwheel fall.

Sam kept his horse to a lope and did not look back. At ten times that distance he did not miss even in poor light.

If Watson or anyone else noticed the muzzleblast they gave no sign of it, but what did ultimately cause confusion was the riderless panicked horse, reins flying, appearing through the chaos.

11

Unexpected Events

Frank Watson, in the centre of a vortex of noise, dust, poor visibility and confusion, had no time to become suspicious even when that riderless horse raced past stirrups flopping. As for the riderless horse, its rider would be neither the first nor last rangeman who was ground to mincemeat during a stampede.

Sam had problems too; it was difficult at any distance to tell horsemen from cattle. He did let the thoroughbred out a notch in order not to lose sight of the turmoil around him, but found no target.

Whatever else Watson was, he was a stockman; stampedes left trampled cows, some with dislocated shoulders and broken legs, and others he would never find. Stampedes were worse even than grass fires, a particular bane, because ground winds drove grass fires at speeds even a fast horse would have trouble staying clear of.

When Sam and Frank Watson met the older man

was riding on a loose rein; he was too far behind to try turning cattle. He was also too sunk in gloom over what this would cost him to heed the shadowy rider coming up on his left side. Sam had recognized Watson from a fair distance but made no attempt to ride stirrup with his enemy until he was satisfied it was indeed the older man.

When he came abreast on Watson's left side he eased the thoroughbred back to match the gait of Watson's horse.

The old man was dolorously wagging his head when he turned to address what he assumed was one of his riders. When their eyes met Watson froze for seconds, then licked thin lips and eased slightly to the right in his saddle.

Sam's six-gun appeared in his lap, aimed and cocked. Watson gently straightened in his saddle, as he asked a foolish question. 'What're you doin' here?'

Sam gestured with the Colt and ignored the question to say, 'Get down!'

Watson drew rein but did not dismount. 'Damned if I will,' he said. 'You'll have to shoot me in my saddle.'

Sam rode a yard or so before speaking again. '*Get down!*'

The old man shook his head, but barely.

Sam eased sideways to grab the old man's reins at the same time the old man went for his holstered Colt.

Sam shot him from his leaning position. The immediate reaction of both horses was a lunging attempt to run in fright. Sam's thoroughbred recovered first and obeyed the reins, but old man

Watson's animal was too terrified by the blinding flash and thunderous sound of a gunshot at close range to respond to control, and Watson, leaning forward, made only a clumsy attempt to stop the horse.

Sam hauled back to a stop, watching and waiting. He only urged his mount ahead when Watson and his animal were beginning to meld with the night, dust and noise.

Where Frank Watson finally left the horse was near an ancient tree of some kind which hadn't rotted but which had for some inexplicable reason hardened as it dried. The horse went up and over it but when it came down, rear end higher than its front end, its rider went off.

Within moments the horse was lost to sight in its terrified run. Sam rode around the deadfall. Watson was pushing to sit up, somewhere during the runaway he had lost his belt gun and his hat.

Sam swung down and stood watching the grizzled older man. Watson had been hit, he knew that, and at close range it had to be a serious injury, but watching the old man struggling on the ground made Sam wonder.

The cattle, scattering in all directions, no longer raised dust where Sam was standing. Even their noise was less.

The old man flopped over and sat up. He cursed Sam in a husky voice. Another time under different circumstances Sam would have been impressed; the old man swore for a full two minutes without once repeating himself.

His hair was awry, his beard-stubbled, lined and weathered face looked sinister in the night. He felt for the belt gun that was not there, spat and began struggling to arise.

Sam watched, leaned and said, 'Your back's broke. You can't get up.'

Watson's fierce gaze did not waver. 'I'll get up,' he said, and would have got close to the deadfall for support when Sam lifted and held him upright, then let go and stepped back.

Watson sank to the ground.

He and Sam exchanged a look before the old man said, 'I should've had you shot, you son of a bitch.'

Sam nodded. 'You should have for a fact,' and hunkered near Watson. 'You're good at that, I expect. Jake Smith—'

'That double-crossin' bastard!'

'He didn't double-cross you. Neither did Will Prescott. They just couldn't hitch horses with you any more.'

'Prescott?'

Sam let that pass. 'Tell me about you'n Mister Carlyle an' the gun-runnin' business.'

Watson looked surprised. 'I don't know what you're talkin' about.'

'I'm gettin' around to why you had Ambrose Saddler shot by Fisher. Because you figured he'd sound off about freightin' guns for you'n Carlyle.'

Watson got closer to the deadfall and leaned against it. If there was pain it could not have been very great, or perhaps Frank Watson was tough enough to ignore it. In either case when he had propped himself he said, 'Art Carlyle's ascairt of his own shadow, the measly, scrawny whelp.'

'Maybe,' Sam replied, and changed the subject

back to the old man's wound. 'I've seen it before, Mister Watson. You'll never walk again, never keep astride a horse.'

Watson's face showed shiny sweat in the weak light. 'I'll walk, an' next time I'll make your wife a widow.'

'Don't have a wife, Mister Watson, an' take my word for it, you'll never have use of your legs again.'

The old man briefly closed his eyes and tilted his head a little. Through clenched teeth he said, 'You're a lousy shot.'

Sam offered no rebuttal. He sat back a little eyeing the old man. Watson was tough, he was dogmatic-stubborn, he was underhanded, mean and murderous, but then, with stampede-thunder miles distant, the night turning chilly, the saddle animals grazing side by side as though they were old acquaintances, and the bitter-faced older man leaning against the log eyes closed, face slightly tilted, Sam felt a touch of pity. He asked how old Watson was and got no answer. He asked if the old man had kin somewhere up north and was answered by the same silence, but eventually Watson lowered his head a tad and opened his eyes. He considered Sam for almost a full minute before saying, 'Ambrose was a flannel-mouthed, drunken, no-good son of a bitch.'

Sam answered curtly. 'So was Al Fisher.'

'No! Al was loyal to the brand. He done what he was told to do. He made a good rangeboss.... Where is he?'

'Dead, Mister Watson. Dead an' buried.'

The old man's fierce gaze showed less anger,

finally, 'Jake, Al ... I saw a riderless horse. Did you shoot him too?'

'Yes.'

'By Gawd I done it wrong, didn't I? When you rode in an' I heard your name ... I did it wrong right from the start. I should've killed you first.'

Sam looked out where the horses were grazing, looked back and saw the old man watching. Watson said, 'Naw, it'd never work. Not if I can't grip with my legs. Leave me here. You're not goin' to take me nowhere an' the longer you set here the better the chance someone'll come back lookin' for me, an' back-shoot you.'

Sam's comment about that was dry. 'Mister Watson, as near as I can figure you only got maybe one rider left, an' he's to hell an' gone with your cattle.'

'Will Prescott?'

'He's on his way out of the country. It's you'n me an' maybe a rider miles from here.'

The old man said, 'Gawdalmighty; a man works hard all his life puttin' things together, an' ends up broke in two against a tree.'

Sam kept his thoughts to himself.

The old man said, 'You got a gun, Saddler, use it.'

Sam went after his horse and led it back to stand in front of Frank Watson. The old man said, 'Use it; you got reason.'

As before Sam did not speak. He snugged up the cinch, shortened the reins and swung astride.

The old man made a rattling sound in his throat and struggled to make his body obey his mind. Sam briefly watched then rode easterly at a walk.

He was about a mile or maybe a little more on his way when he heard the gunshot, which was about as long as he thought it would take Frank Watson to drag himself where his six-gun had been dropped.

The night was turning cold, the moon was gone and the stars looked watery-weak, a slight ground breeze made intermittent passes across the dead quiet land. When he reached the stage road he turned south.

He could only estimate how far he was from town and his guess was that he had a long way to go. He let the thoroughbred slog along on loose reins.

There was still one more.

The ground breeze built up over time to a fair wind. Sam had it in his face and rode hunched. The thoroughbred was less bothered, it was insulated against both wind and cold.

He dozed in the saddle, missed seeing several lights until the tall horse blew its nose and roused him. Saddler's Wells was dead to the world. He speculated about the few lights; mothers with croupy kids or oldsters burning oil all night just in case.

He rode down the centre of a place that could have been devoid of people, turned in at the livery barn, dismounted stiffly and led his horse out front of the harness room, where it stood patiently until divested of riding gear and was led to a stall, then it fretted.

Sam climbed to the loft, pitched down a manger full of timothy, climbed down to grain the animal, then went out back to stand in chilly, dark silence for a spell before returning to the loft ladder and climbing up.

Wind scrabbled at eave-ends and bumbled over the roof. Sam shed what he had to, burrowed into the hay, listened to boards rattling and wondered who would get old man Watson's cattle, horses and laden wagon. He also wondered wherever the old man's ranch was – who would get that? Just before falling asleep he thought the comparison between snuffing out a candle and exiting this life were pretty close to the same; folks had to pick up the wax from the candle – and glean what they found of the accumulation of worldly goods from the Frank Watsons who would have no need.

What eventually awakened him was Rattlesnake down below whistling the old Secesh marching song called 'Lorena'. He was working clear of the timothy in order to stand up and find his hat, boots, shellbelt and sidearm when he heard someone speak down below in a cranky voice. Rattlesnake's reply was clear.

'Two days, Doc. Three at the most,' and the medicine man's annoyed response. 'If I'd said two, three days, you'd have said four, five days.'

Rattlesnake's ability at defusing potential arguments made him say, 'It bothers me, Doc. He could be dead or hurt bad-off somewhere beyond help.'

Doc's answer this time was more disgusted than annoyed. 'No one who rides into five *arrieros* or whatever they was, an' kills four without a scratch is likely to be needin' help. If he comes in let me know; better yet I'll return after breakfast. He'll turn up, Rattlesnake. Bad pennies always do.'

Sam finished shedding hay, dropped his hat on,

turned and began the backward climb down from
the loft. When he was on solid earth Rattlesnake was
standing like he'd taken root.

Sam said, 'Good mornin'. I'll go join Doc at the
eatery,' and walked past Rattlesnake who neither
moved nor made a sound, but when the shock
passed he went along stall doors until he found the
thoroughbred.

The sun was climbing; Saddler's Wells was going
about its business, and most of the Chinee's customers had breakfasted at least an hour earlier.
Except for Doctor Morton there was one old tooth-
less gaffer drinking from a bowl of soup. He made
the only noise as Sam lowered himself to the bench
beside Doctor Morton, who stared as Rattlesnake
had done, but in the medical man's case the shock
passed more quickly.

The caféman put two cups of black java on the
counter and returned to his cooking area. Breakfast
was always the same at the Chinee's eatery, tough
broiled steak, mashed potatoes, a piece of buttered
toast hard enough to roll over rocks without
cracking, and jelly the colour of mud made in the
Chinee's kitchen.

Doc settled forward ignoring Sam. The old gaffer
finished his soup, used the cuff of an ancient coat to
wipe his lower face, put down a nickel and smiled at
Sam on his way out. 'Goin' to be a nice day,' he said.

Doc waited until the door had closed behind the
old man then said, 'It's about time. For me there
hasn't been a nice day in weeks, an' where'n hell you
been? That cousin of yours has got Widow Harris
eatin' out of his hand. He's trouble four ways from
the middle.'

'How's his wound?'

Doc turned a sour face. 'How would I know? I haven't seen it since you left. Widow Harris took over carin' for it – an' your cousin.'

Their platters arrived, the caféman fixed them both with challenging black eyes. Sam said, 'It looks mighty good,' and the caféman went back to his kitchen, somewhat mollified. For some reason he could not understand his customers complaining endlessly and loudly, until he retreated to his cooking area then they broke out into loud, rough laughter.

Doc made a remark that caught Sam's attention. 'There's soldiers in the country.'

Sam stopped chewing. 'Soldiers?'

'The whip on the north-bound coach from down in the Borderton country saw 'em yestiddy. One of them patrols I expect. Hasn't been no hostile war-whoops around for ten years.'

Sam went back to his meal. When he finished he offered a suggestion. 'If there's a ruckus down in Messico the army'd most likely be patrollin' to keep the losers out.'

Doc was hunched around his coffee cup. 'I haven't heard of no revolution down there. No one else I've talked to has, either.'

'Just a routine patrol.'

Doc shrugged, twisted and put a bleak gaze on Sam. 'You goin' down to see your cousin?'

'Yes.'

'Well ... good luck.'

Sam got sidetracked in front of the eatery by a stone-faced individual he would have thought he would never see again. Prescott's tan-tawny eyes barely showed recognition. He said, 'Did you get it done?'

Sam nodded.

'The old man...?'

'Shot himself.'

'*What!*'

Sam explained and the tawny-eyed man stared without speaking for several seconds, then he nodded. 'I guess that'd be about how he'd go out. I wouldn't want to stay around with legs I'd have to drag. What about the cattle?'

'I don't know. Last I heard they was better'n a mile off an' still runnin'.' As Sam finished speaking he put his head slightly to one side. 'I'd guess if a man was handy enough he could round up what he could find an' claim 'em.'

Prescott's gaze did not leave Sam's face and again he was slow to speak, but when he did he gently nodded and said, 'You put a bee in my bonnet, Mister Saddler.'

Sam's reply was quietly given. 'A man's got to start somewhere; recognize opportunity when he sees it. Or he can keep ridin' south. Good luck, Mister Prescott.'

The tawny-eyed man watched Sam cross the road and leaned against an upright out front of the eatery. The leather man was right; opportunities for a man to get set up on his own didn't happen often. In fact during William Prescott's forty-odd years they had never happened before.

Widow Harris met Sam at the door. He was not sure whether her expression was of pleasure at his return, or uneasiness because of his return.

She took him to the empty parlour before she

said, 'Emory's on the mend. He's healthy as a horse. I've taken over mindin' him.' She smoothed the apron in her lap as she said, 'You can go up, he'll be glad to see you.'

When Sam entered the bedroom the first thing he saw was curtains on the window that had not been there before. The second thing was his cousin propped up on pillows reading a book. As a youngster Emory had roared like a boar bear when he'd been forced to read. He dropped the book and greeted Sam with a broad smile and a shout. He said, 'I'd about give up on you. Another two, three days then I was goin' to go lookin' for you.'

Sam pulled a chair close to the little bedside table with a large glass bowl full of fruit. Sam was sarcastic. 'I wouldn't expect you to leave here, unless you maybe waited a month. How's the leg?'

Emory impulsively flung back the blankets. The leg was down to normal size and had been freshly bandaged. Sam was impressed. 'I never saw Doc make that neat a bandage.'

'He didn't do it, Eunice did. She's right handy.' As Emory pulled the blankets back up he said, 'Sam, I been thinkin'.'

Sam's reply was dourly said, 'I'll bet you have.'

As though there had been no interruption his cousin said, 'Me'n Eunice got to be good friends. She can cook up a storm an' she's lonely. Her husband—'

'Emory, do you want to know what happened when I went after the men who shot you?'

'Yes. I figured when you come through that door that it got settled your way or you wouldn't be here.'

'You want to know what happened?'

'Yes sir, I really do, but right now Eunice'll be showin' up with a tray and fresh java....'

Sam arose, squeezed past the widow woman coming up the same set of stairs he was going down, and sure enough she was not only carrying a tray of food but there was a skimpy little vase with a damned flower in it.

12

For Better or Worse

Doc was right about the soldiers. Late of a weekday afternoon they rode into Saddler's Wells, dusty, faded, unsmiling and tired.

Their officer went down to Rattlesnake's barn to make arrangements for horse care, and Rattlesnake agreed to corral, feed and look after the army animals but he did not do it happily. Over the years he'd done business with the army and was invariably paid with vouchers which had to be forwarded to the War Department in Washington to be paid, something which seemed to take forever but which actually took several months.

Soldiers in Saddler's Wells were a novelty. To the best of local recollections there hadn't been blue uniforms in town in more than eight or ten years.

Because Sam's leather works was located at the north end of town he did not know soldiers had ridden in until the big Greek bellowed about it from the duckboards in front of his saloon.

Sam had reason to be anxious. For one thing he had fought a private vendetta to its bloody conclusion, something the law, as a rule, did not condone. The other reason was based on the fact that, unlike states of the Federal Union which had their own law-enforcement establishments, territories which had not been as yet admitted to the Federal Union were classified as Territories, and territories where governed by the army, meant martial law.

He stood in the doorway of his shop watching as an officer and a grizzled, red-faced sergeant entered the saloon. Within moments he heard the Greek disputing the army's right of enforcing martial law.

Sam shed his apron and crossed the road. When he entered, the Greek loudly said that the leather man was one of Saddler's Wells prominent citizens. The soldiers turned to make their judgement as Sam approached the bar. When Spartas resumed his tirade Sam looked steadily at him. Chris's tirade died. He made a wide sweep of the bar and went to wait on several townsmen. Sam and the officer exchanged looks as the officer said, 'You know him pretty well, do you, Mister Saddler?'

Sam grinned. 'Well enough. His bark's worse'n his bite.'

The soldier extended a hand. 'Captain Elias Lee. No; no relation to Robert E.'

Sam shook and released the extended hand. He and the grizzled three-stripe campaigner exchanged a nod but there was no introduction.

The officer offered to stand drinks. Sam shook his head. 'I'm not much of a drinkin' man,' he said, 'but go right ahead if you gents are of a mind.'

The sergeant had the bottle. He tipped the officer's little glass full then did the same for himself, but unlike the officer, who made no move to touch the glass, the sergeant threw back his head, downed the jolt and watched the Greek as the officer asked questions, most of which Sam answered without difficulty. When the captain asked about Arthur Carlyle, Sam eyed him closely. 'Owns the mercantile. I guess he's been here some years.'

'Do you know him personally?'

'To speak to is about all.'

Captain Lee nodded his head in the Greek's direction. 'We heard that when you came to Saddler's Wells you shot it out with some *bandoleros*.'

Sam nodded. 'They'd been trailin' me. I had the town in sight when I made a run at them.'

'The way I heard it you killed four and the fifth one ran.'

Sam nodded. 'They'd been doggin' me. I know their kind. Wait for the right time an' place an' set up a bushwhack.'

The captain gazed dispassionately at Sam. 'Big odds, Mister Saddler.'

'It wasn't my choice, Captain.'

'Mister Saddler, they weren't dogging you.'

Sam softly frowned. 'They sure as hell gave me that impression, Captain.'

The officer almost imperceptibly shook his head. 'They were coming to Saddler's Wells. My guess is that they followed you because they an' you were going in the same direction.'

Sam was sceptical. 'A coincidence?'

'Not exactly. I'd like to get back to Mister Carlyle. Have you any idea that he might be in the business of selling guns to Mexicans down over the line?'

Sam was beginning to have an idea. He said, 'I've heard that. Him an' a cowman named Watson.'

'Mister Saddler, those *bandoleros* you shot were coming to Saddler's Wells to drive a pair of wagons down to Mexico. The rigs were loaded with contraband guns.'

Sam considered his face in the back-bar mirror briefly before speaking again. 'Why'n hell did they dog me? They could've rode ahead or laid back.'

Lee had no explanation. 'I don't know. What I do know is that they were coming here to take over the loaded rigs an' drive them down into Mexico.'

Sam had a question of his own. 'You got a good reason for figurin' that, Captain?'

Lee smiled. 'The four you shot up an' the one that escaped made it necessary for the trader down in Mexico to send up four more to drive the wagons over the line for him. On our sweep across the line from east to west, we caught four *bandoleros* in camp. We surrounded them in the night. Some of my men speak Spanish. The *bandoleros* were talking about finding you and killing you before they took delivery of the wagons.' Lee showed that thin smile again. 'We took them without firing a shot. Three of my company have them tied like turkeys where we made our last camp. They didn't hold back. We even have the name of the trader down in Mexico they were to deliver the guns to – and the name of the *gringo* up here who bought the guns up north, brought them to Saddler's Wells to keep until the *bandoleros* arrived to drive the wagons back.'

Sam let go a quiet long breath. 'You got Carlyle?' he asked and Lee shook his head. 'We found the wagons in his shed out back. Mister Saddler, I got no idea how he did it, but one of those wagons has a Gatling gun in it.'

Sam was impressed. 'I'd guess that'd bring a lot of money in Messico.'

Lee let that pass. 'Gatling guns are army property. A man can't walk into a store an' buy one. But that's the army's affair, how he got the gun and who the person was that sold it to him – and where *he* got it. Right now I want Mister Carlyle.'

Sam's retort was as dry as old corn husks. 'I expect you do. Have you been to the store?'

'Yes. It's locked up.'

'His house?'

'We went there. He wasn't around, and before you ask if we went to see his clerk, I can tell you the clerk had no idea where Carlyle might have gone. There's something else. Maybe you could help us. A cowman named—'

'Frank Watson?'

'Yes.'

'He's dead.'

'You're sure?'

'I was there. He shot himself.'

'Why? From what I've gathered he was a tough individual, hard as iron.'

'He shot himself because his back was broke an' given the kind of man he was, the idea of havin' to drag his legs for the rest of his life wasn't worth it.'

'You're sure of this, Mister Saddler?'

'I told you, I was there.'

'Where did this happen?'

'About a day's ride north an' a tad west where he made a night camp in a little meadow.'

Captain Lee finally hoisted his jolt glass, emptied it and jerked his head. 'Take a little hike with me, Mister Saddler.'

The sergeant waited until the spindle doors stopped moving before signalling for Chris Spartas to refill his glass.

Captain Lee cut through a dog trot to the alley on the east side of town. Carlyle's storage facility had at one time been a very large barn. The wooden siding was warped and weathered to streaked brown. Captain Lee wrestled one large door open. It was blacker than the inside of a well but the officer led the way as though he had previously been there, which indeed he had.

Both large wagons had their tongues up off the ground atop small kegs. Tarps had been tied well on both sides of each wagon. The tarp Captain Lee flung back had not been retied from his earlier visit. He stepped back and gestured for Sam to climb atop the massive rear wheel, which Sam did, and despite poor light he made out the rifle crates – and a Gatling gun near the high tailgate which appeared to be fully assembled, except for the top-loading magazine.

Sam climbed down, wiped his hands and followed the officer out into the night where they both leaned to close the sagging door.

Sam said, 'Son of a bitch! How long's this gun-runnin' business been goin' on?'

'According to one of the *bandoleros*, who had made many trips up and back, it's been goin' on for maybe four, five years. And, Mister Saddler, whatever the partnership between Carlyle and Watson amounted to, I'd guess they both made fortunes. That Gatling gun by itself would fetch maybe, five, six thousand dollars to *pronunciados* in Mexico. In a revolution a gun like that, or several like that, could mean the difference between winning and losing.'

Sam considered the backs of several buildings before saying, 'Rattlesnake would know if Carlyle got his horse.'

He led the way back through the dog trot and on a diagonal course to the livery barn.

Rattlesnake was sleeping on a tipped-back chair with both booted feet atop an unkempt, scarred and battered desk. When Sam shook his shoulder Rattlesnake almost lost his balance and went over backwards.

Sam steadied him as he asked his question, and Rattlesnake answered while rubbing his eyes. 'His buggy animal was here an hour ago. Let's go see.'

The particular animal they sought was kept stalled and day-sheeted by Mister Carlyle's orders. As they leaned on the lower half of the door the horse awakened and blinked its eyes at them.

As they turned away Sam said, 'Damned fool. He should've taken wing when he saw blue-bellies in town.'

Rattlesnake, finally wide awake, made an innocent statement. 'He likely didn't see 'em. He went over to the widow's place after supper.'

Sam led the way again, and when Widow Harris opened the door her eyes widened at the sight of a soldier. She wordlessly led them to the parlour, which was empty for a change, and scarcely saw them seated when Sam asked about his cousin. Widow Harris, for some unknown reason, blushed and avoided Sam's gaze as she replied, 'He's on the mend. Had a little touch of croup so I had him breathe vinegar an' water vapours. He's a hard man to keep down, Mister Saddler. After supper he swore he heard someone downstairs an' wanted to get out of bed to go see.' Widow Harris rolled her eyes. 'I had a time convincin' him there was no one downstairs. I got no overnights now. Maybe it was rats; these wood houses get rats no matter—'

Sam interrupted, 'Have you seen Mister Carlyle this evenin'?'

'No. I haven't seen him for the last day or two. It's not like it used to be. He still pays me to keep a place for him but—'

'A room?' Sam asked.

'Well, he uses a room upstairs from time to time but Mister Carlyle an' my late husband set up a still in the cellar. Now'n then he goes down there but I made it clear after my husband passed on, there's to be no more whiskey-makin' in this house.'

Sam stood up. 'I didn't know you had a cellar.'

As the widow also arose she said since the passing of her husband she kept the door locked, and since he had died some years before Sam came to Saddler's Wells there was no reason for him to know about the cellar.

Sam asked for the key and Widow Harris stared. 'Whatever for? There's nothin' down there but that still an' the empty mash barrel an' a bottle capper'n the like.'

Sam tried again. 'How do you get down there?'

'There's an outside door around back, but I had

it boarded up. Otherwise there's the door from the hallway.'

'Is it locked?'

'Yes. I don't go down there.'

Sam did not ask where the door was, he went along the hall until he found it. The lock was in place but when he lifted it the curved top was loose in his hand. He handed the lock to the widow woman, jerked his head at the captain, opened the door and saw nothing but darkness down a flight of stairs. He led the way again, this time using his left hand to feel the wall during his descent.

Captain Lee asked the widow for a lamp. She went to the kitchen and returned with a lantern. Captain Lee started down the stairs shedding light as he descended.

The aroma was undeniable although faint; whiskey had been made in the cellar.

It had evidently long been used for discarded furniture as well as assorted sizes of boxes, haphazardly stacked as though whoever had brought them down here shoved boxes wherever he could, probably in haste.

As with most storage areas it was a jumble of odds and ends except where the still stood. That area had been cleared of everything not essential to the making of white lightning.

Sam moved silently. Captain Lee was midway down the stairs with his lantern when a well-aimed gunshot shattered the lamp. The captain fell, swore and fumbled in spilt lamp oil to regain his upright position.

Sam was groping in darkness when he heard what could have been scurrying rats. He had his six-gun in one hand as he said, 'Give it up, Carlyle. The only way out is the stairs and—'

He did not get to finish. Again the captain swore but this time oil-slippery steps were less of a problem for him than the headlong rush of a man up the stairs.

They both fell.

Sam hurried to the base of the stairs. What little light came from the open hall doorway made it possible for him to see both men. One, the officer, was larger. The other man was wiry and agile. He recovered first and would have continued his desperate rush up the oily steps if Sam hadn't rushed him, got one trouser leg and threw his weight backward. The wiry man twisted. Sam saw the pistol coming around and dropped flat. The second gunshot tore the still's copper coils loose.

Sam fired from the floor. The sinewy man spun and lunged to get up to the door. He fell short, rolled until he knocked the legs from under Captain Lee, who fell again.

Sam called to the wiry shadow. 'Don't move, I'll blow your gawddamn head off!'

A little bleating noise was the only sound after Sam fell silent.

Captain Lee was upright again. He drew his holstered army handgun and cocked it. The bleating was interrupted by a shrill whine. 'Don't shoot! I give up!'

Lee asked Sam to move where the officer could see him, which Sam did. The captain groped his way until his foot came in contact with something that yielded. He leaned far over, aimed his cocked Colt. This time the bleating voice spoke so swiftly the words ran together.

'I surrender! I give up! Don't shoot – please!'

Sam had no difficulty recognizing the voice, even though it was high pitched with fright. He said, 'Stand up, Mister Carlyle.'

Someone from the doorway above called profanely and Sam's retort was curt. 'Get out of the damned doorway, Emory!'

The light from above showed again. Sam heard a woman's pleading voice which he ignored as he felt for the sinewy man's shirt and pushed him in the direction of the stairs. The captain followed. He was limping.

Sam kept his grip on Carlyle's collar all the way upstairs where his cousin and the widow woman were staring like statues.

The men from the basement smelled strongly of the coal oil with which each of them had been smeared.

Widow Harris found her tongue. 'Take him to the kitchen. I don't want lamp oil on my floors.'

Sam punched the storekeeper where there was bright light and shoved him down on a chair. Captain Lee favoured one leg as he leaned on the wall. Emory appeared, tousle-headed, wrapped in a robe which was too small, and squinted at Sam. 'What in the hell...?'

Sam was wiping off coal oil when he answered. 'That there is Captain Lee. He wants Mister Carlyle for gun runnin'.' Sam twisted to gaze at the sinewy, seated man. 'Why'n hell didn't you get a horse and hightail it?'

The reply he got was enlightening. 'My buggy mare isn't broke to ride an' I didn't know any of the other horses.'

Emory was puzzled. 'Are you scairt of horses?'

Carlyle nodded his head and Emory rolled his eyes as the widow woman tugged at his sleeve. 'You shouldn't have come down those stairs!'

'With someone firing a gun in the house?'

'For no reason. Now come along.' She pushed and punched Emory in the direction of the stairs leading to his room. The men in the kitchen could hear her scolding all the way.

Captain Lee addressed Arthur Carlyle. 'For running contraband, Mister Carlyle, you could do ten years stockade time. Where did you get that Gatling gun?'

'From two soldiers up at Fort Shilling.'

Lee nodded grimly as he eased more weight off his sore leg. 'We'll take care of that. Mister Carlyle you're under military arrest. Stand up!'

Sam had lost track of time, but the moment he, the prisoner and the soldier got outside where the cold hit him, he guessed, correctly, it was close to dawn.

Two days later Captain Lee led his troopers and his prisoners back southward. For Sam getting back to his leather works was thoroughly agreeable. One thing mildly annoyed him: his congenial, wanderlust cousin told Sam he and the Widow Harris figured to be married before the end of summer. Sam liked his cousin, but liked him best from a distance.

It added little to Sam's enjoyment of life that Doc Morton's daughter Marianne returned from her visit to the South, and renewed her interest in Sam until the day Doc came storming into the leather works mad as a wet hen. Marianne had run off with a travelling salesman who wore a curly-brimmed derby hat, yellow spats over his shoes and wore a glass ring big enough to choke a horse which he swore was a diamond.

It was early autumn when a steady-eyed lanky man came to the shop to have a saddle made to his specifications. He and Sam exchanged a long blank look as the stockman, whose name was William Prescott, dryly said he had rebranded close to 300 head of FW cattle and was fixing to set up in the cow business on land he'd bought north-west of town.